BOSS WITH BENEFITS

A SECRET BABY ROMANCE

CRYSTAL MONROE

CHAPTER 1

JACK

"*N*o, don't pull your account. We can fix this!" I shouted into the phone.

But it was too late. The client had already hung up. Correction: *former* client.

"Kate, give me another one!" I called down the hall to the receptionist. Normally, my executive assistant would transfer my calls. But since I'd fired my EA the day before, that wasn't going to happen.

"Just pick any line!" Kate said, sounding near tears.

All the lights on my phone flashed angrily. My chest felt tight as I looked at them all, trying not to panic. This company was my baby. I had to save it.

"Which line is the highest-priority client?" I shouted down the hall desperately.

"They're all high priority!" Kate said between sobs. She was now openly crying. That meant we'd lost another client.

Shit!

"The bug has been fixed," I assured the next client on the line. "There won't be another security breach."

"So you say. There never should have been one in the first place," the client blustered.

"The data breach was very minor," I explained. "Only your employees' last names were leaked."

"A breach is a breach, Jack," he said. "I'm taking my business elsewhere."

I couldn't blame him for being angry. A cybersecurity company needed to guarantee its services. The clients' loss of data was unacceptable. Worst of all, it was my fault.

As the owner and CEO of Lion, Inc., I should have realized that my executive assistant was in *way* over her head. She was making mistakes on a regular basis. A disaster was inevitable. I should have fired her long ago, but I was a day too late. Now everyone was paying the price.

My partner and co-CEO, Grayson, stuck his head in my door. He looked as bad as I felt. "I lost two more clients, but I managed to save one," he said.

My stomach tightened. If we lost two out of every three clients, the company that we'd built together would be ruined.

"We can't afford to lose many more," I said.

"Everyone's pissed off," he said, shaking his head. "And this is just a minor breach. I'd hate to see how they'd act if their bank accounts were compromised."

I shuddered at the thought. He returned to his office as I took the next call.

Grayson and I had known each other since we partnered up in computer class in middle school. We'd been buddies ever since. Together, we'd developed our cybersecurity system when we were a couple of broke kids in college.

We'd worked our asses off to launch Lion. After a rocky beginning, the business had shot off like a rocket. And over the years, it had been successful beyond our wildest dreams.

But today, I was in danger of losing it all thanks to my

own stupidity. I never should have hired such an inexperienced assistant. And now that I'd fired her, I didn't have anyone to help clean up the mess she'd left.

I spent the morning calming angry clients, using my persuasive skills to smooth things over. I ended up giving away a huge portion of our revenue in free services. But I was able to save enough of our clients to keep the company afloat.

"We did it," I said with an exhausted sigh as Grayson sat across from me at my desk.

"No, *you* did it." He slugged me on the shoulder. "I struck out with almost every client I spoke to. Because of you, Lion will live another day."

"And if I'd hired a better assistant, we'd never have been in this mess in the first place," I groaned. But there was no time for looking back. That wasn't my style. I believed in action. Clapping my hands together, I said energetically, "I'm going to replace all those clients we lost, starting right now."

Grayson nodded. "I'll go check in with the programmers to make sure the code's still working." He left my office looking a little more upbeat.

I made a list of potential clients, then cracked my knuckles and picked up the phone. I'd call the IT director of each company and lay on the patented Jack McCann charm.

"Aren't you the company that had the breach yesterday?" the first contact on the list asked after I introduced myself.

My heart fell. I did everything I could to convince him the issue was resolved and wouldn't happen again, but it didn't matter.

"I just can't risk signing with you guys." He hung up.

I fought the urge to punch the desk in frustration. That was the kind of reaction my father would have, and I'd vowed long ago never to be like that son-of-a-bitch.

In fact, Dad's violent rages had given me the idea for the company years ago.

Whenever he was in one of his moods, I got out of his way. Grayson let me hide out in his parents' garage during my father's drinking binges. During those times, I started thinking about protecting what was really important.

I thought about the people who worked themselves to death to keep food on the table and a roof over their kids' heads. The world was full of predators who would use technology to take advantage. They'd hack into credit card companies, banks, and employee databases, stealing their identities and their money right out from under them.

I couldn't make the world a safe place, but maybe I could help people not lose everything to assholes online.

So, using cheap laptops and our ingenuity, Grayson and I developed a system to protect companies from the hyenas of the world.

Now, I sat in a cozy office as CEO and owner. I managed a staff of programmers and software engineers, in addition to the administrative workers. At the age of thirty-four, I was living the sweet life in Beverly Hills, with a huge house in the city and a new vacation house on the beach. Not bad for a poor kid from an abusive home.

But if we didn't get some new clients, it would all go up in smoke.

With a sigh, I crossed the first contact off the list and started dialing the next number.

My receptionist, Kate, stuck her head in the door. "Excuse me, Mr. McCann. Your one o'clock is here."

"What one o'clock?" I snapped.

"You scheduled an interview for the executive assistant position today at one," Kate said. Suddenly, the memory came flooding back to me.

I gritted my teeth and hung up the phone. "Fine, send

her in."

Shit! This was the worst possible time for an interview. Filling the assistant position was a priority, no doubt. But first, I needed to finish cleaning up the mess the last one had made.

This applicant had been recommended to me by my realtor, of all people. Stuart Kline. When he'd delivered the keys for my new beach house to my office the day before, he'd overheard me putting an ad out for the position.

"You should interview my friend for the job," he'd said. "She's an experienced assistant."

He'd spoken of her with so much enthusiasm I couldn't refuse.

"Sure," I'd said. "Have her come in tomorrow right after lunch."

That was before I knew half my clients were about to leave.

I was tempted to turn her away, but she was already here. I might as well conduct the interview. Besides, I could use a break from getting kicked in the balls with every phone call.

I sat up straight in my chair as the door opened. A stunningly gorgeous woman walked in wearing a floral dress. She was in her mid-twenties and petite, with an incredible hourglass figure complete with full breasts, a tiny waist, and a luscious ass I wanted to bite like a piece of ripe fruit.

Her face was beautiful, with a wholesome farm girl quality I found refreshing, minimal make-up, and the most stunning violet-gray eyes I'd ever seen. Her chestnut brown hair fell to her shoulders in rich waves, and her smile was pure sunlight.

"Hello, Mr. McCann. I'm Violet Williams." She introduced herself with a confident handshake and handed me her résumé. "Thank you for seeing me today. I know I'd be a terrific asset to Lion, Inc."

"What makes you think that?" I asked, intrigued by her.

She ran through her qualifications, and I was surprised that she had ample education and experience relevant to the job. But I had to remind myself to focus on her words and not her lips. I couldn't stop gawking at how incredibly attractive she was. Those wide hips flaring out from her narrow waist... An image of my hands on those curves flashed in my mind.

Down, boy, I told myself. Even if I hired this woman, there was no chance of anything unprofessional happening between us. The number one rule of being a CEO was never to get involved with an employee. I had plenty of eager and willing women in my contacts I could call when I was horny.

"This is a letter of recommendation from my last employer," she said. She handed me another paper from the folder she carried. My eyes grazed over her tiny, delicate hands, and I shifted in my seat, forcing myself to look away.

I skimmed the document. It was full of glowing praise for her. She seemed competent, but I had to make sure she could handle the workload.

I started hammering Violet with questions. I didn't mean to come across like the Spanish Inquisition, but I couldn't go easy on her just because she was hot.

To my surprise, Violet answered each question with intelligence, poise, and wit. Nothing shook her. I was secretly impressed, but I didn't let her see that.

"I work long hours. You'll be required to come in early, stay late, work weekends, and even holidays," I stated firmly. Hearing myself, I realized I was coming off like a real hard-ass jerk, but I'd found it was better to be honest and upfront than to surprise an employee later with the harsh realities of the job.

"Not a problem. I'm available anytime," Violet said with a smile.

Her lips were soft and pink. I wanted desperately to kiss them.

I locked my eyes on hers, refusing to let myself look anywhere else. "Tell me about you personally. What motivates you?"

"Mostly, getting out of my hometown," she said and laughed nervously. I felt myself grow hard as she crossed her legs. "I grew up in rural Iowa. It's a nice place, but it wasn't for me. I couldn't do the kind of work I love in my town, for one thing. I enjoy administrative support work, to be honest. It's kind of my thing—helping a company run like clockwork. I love learning everything I can about business."

Her face lit up as she talked about her passion for building a successful career.

"So, I came to LA determined to make my dream come true, and nothing is going to stop me," she said with fire in her eyes.

I saw a kindred spirit in her. She was smart, driven, and eloquent – a perfect fit for the company. Still, hiring an employee who wasn't up to the job was what got me in trouble the last time. I had to be tough with this one.

"I expect everyone who works for me to give this company one hundred and ten percent, just like I do every damn day," I stated firmly. "This isn't some nine-to-five job you can half-ass."

I recited my speech designed to root out anyone who wasn't truly dedicated. Usually, applicants squirmed in their seats, but not Violet. She kept her gorgeous eyes fixed on me. I felt mesmerized by them. Almost hypnotized.

"I need an executive assistant who can do this job with concrete precision," I stated with finality, hoping she wouldn't notice I'd gotten lost in my speech.

"Well, it's a good thing I've got my cement mixer parked out back," Violet said with a sassy smile.

In spite of myself, I cracked a tiny chuckle. It was the first time I'd laughed since this whole mess with the breach had begun.

"Let me assure you, Mr. McCann, I'll give everything I've got to this job," she said. "Hire me, and you'll see what a great asset I can be to this company."

Looking at Violet, I realized that beyond her intelligence, she was amazingly brave. I liked an employee who wasn't afraid to stand up for herself. I needed someone sharp to keep me on my toes.

"All right, Ms. Williams. You can start tomorrow. But be warned, I expect the very best."

"Don't worry, Mr. McCann. You'll get my best every day. Thank you!" She beamed, making her look even more beautiful.

I would have walked her to the door, but because of my raging hard-on, I couldn't. Instead, I reached across my desk to extend my hand, and she leaned close to shake it farewell. She smelled like a garden, and I breathed in her scent as she turned and walked toward the door. Suddenly, she turned back toward me and gave me a shy smile.

"Thank you so much for the job. You won't be sorry!" she said eagerly. Then she turned and left.

I blew out a breath and pulled at my tie. I had a hunch she'd be great at the job. And I was in desperate need of help.

But I still worried I'd regret hiring her. After all, could I really work with someone I found so incredibly fucking attractive?

I ran a hand through my hair and turned to look out the window at the street below.

If I was going to work with such a sexy assistant, I'd have to push my feelings aside. For the sake of my company, I hoped I could.

"Thank you! Thank you! Thank you!" I cried out repeatedly as I wrapped my arms around my roommate in a hug.

"You got the job?" Stuart asked me, and I nodded vigorously. He cheered and took my hands as we jumped up and down together. "You got the job! Congratulations!"

"All thanks to you, Stuart!" I exclaimed, letting him go to catch my breath. "You're the one who got me that interview."

"But you're the one who aced the interview, silly. I knew you could do it!"

"That makes one of us," I sighed. We made our way to the living room of the second-floor apartment I shared with Stuart. I plopped on the stylish couch beside him.

"Now, don't start letting your parents get back into your head," Stuart chastised with a wave of his finger.

"You're right. But when you're told your whole life that your only possible future will be standing in a kitchen barefoot and pregnant, you start to doubt your abilities," I said. "Don't get me wrong. I want a family someday, but I want the chance to have a career first. And hopefully, this job will be the first step toward that goal."

"Sweetie, that's exactly why I rescued you from that middle-of-nowhere town in Iowa we both grew up in," Stuart said, putting his feet up on the coffee table. He always wore the latest fashions, and today he was decked out in a striped button-down shirt with turquoise pants. Only Stuart could pull off pants like that. "You thought you had it rough being told you had to get a husband? Imagine how I felt being told I had to get a wife! I knew my parents would never accept having a gay son. Which is exactly when I moved to Los Angeles and never looked back."

"Well, that's not entirely true," I pointed out. "You looked back enough to keep inviting me to move out here with you."

"True," Stuart said with a feisty tilt of his head, his cropped blond hair staying perfectly in place. "The question is, what on earth took you so long? I've been here five years, slogging my way up the real estate chain, building my client base. I started off as a nobody, and now I've just sold my biggest property ever—a beach house to a millionaire mogul of cybersecurity. For some reason, you didn't agree to move out here with me till last year."

"I guess I was in denial longer than you were." I shrugged, twirling a strand of my long brown hair. "I kept hoping Mom and Dad would realize I wanted to do something different with my life, especially when I took all those business classes at the community college. But I realized they never would the day I got my business degree. That was when Mom said to me, 'I'm glad you got *that* out of your system.' Then they started inviting Mark Hansen over for dinner every night, hinting at what a great married couple we'd make."

"That hick farmer with the big ears?" Stuart rolled his eyes in disgust. "I forgot about him. Your children would have looked like Dumbo."

"It didn't help that my younger sister was already married with two children. I got so sick of hearing my parents say, 'Why can't you be more like Jessica?' I love my sister, but I'm not ready for marriage and kids until I get a chance to have a career first. So, when Jessica told me she spotted Mark shopping for an engagement ring, I knew I had to get out of there. That night, I started planning my escape. And soon after that, I bought my bus ticket for LA."

"And I went to the bus station to pick you up and brought you home like a little lost puppy," Stuart said, exaggerating the dreamy far-off look of someone recalling a fond memory.

"Shut up! I was not a lost puppy." I shoved him on the shoulder like only best friends can do. "I arrived in LA as an independent woman ready to make my dreams come true."

"Until you met loser boy." Stuart rolled his eyes dramatically.

"Ugh, don't remind me!" I grabbed one of the throw pillows from the sofa and hit him with it. "How was I supposed to know that Nathan was going to turn out to be such a jerk?"

"Oh, I don't know. Maybe the way you always had to pay for dinner? Or how about the time he forgot to pick you up from work because he was playing video games? You were more like his mother than his girlfriend, always doing his laundry and cooking his meals."

"Okay, I get it," I said with a laugh. I didn't like having my obvious mistake thrown in my face, but I knew Stuart was doing it out of love. "At least I only wasted six months of my life dating Nathan. If I had married Mark Hansen, I would've been stuck till death do us part."

"You need to find a real man. Someone smart, and rich, and sexy. Someone who really knows how to treat a woman." Stuart's eyes glistened as he picked up a magazine from the coffee table and held it up dramatically for me to see. "Someone like this!"

I gasped as I saw the cover was a photo of none other than my new boss, Jack McCann. The banner *Sexiest CEO Bachelor* was emblazoned across the front in bold red letters.

"Give me that!" I grabbed at the magazine, but Stuart held it out of my reach as he read the article aloud, taunting me.

"'Jack McCann, owner and creator of the cybersecurity company Lion, Inc., isn't just a powerful CEO. He's also one of LA's sexiest and most eligible bachelors. The multi-millionaire can often be seen partying at LA's hottest bars and clubs, drinking aged scotch and dancing with some of Hollywood's hottest actresses and models. His massive estate has plenty of room for a family, and yet he remains stead-fastly unattached, having never been involved in a serious romantic relationship. His sexy blue eyes, thick dark hair, and muscular physique have this reporter asking the ques-tion, is there a woman out there who can tame this stallion and get him to settle down?'"

Stuart snapped the magazine closed as he finished reading and fanned himself with it. He said teasingly, "This article says it all. It's too bad he's straight, but that's why I offered him up to you. Tell me, was he everything I said he would be at the interview or what?"

"No, not at all." I glared at Stuart vehemently. "He was rude, condescending, and basically a complete ass."

"Yeah, but what a fine-looking ass it is!" Stuart smacked his lips, and I couldn't help but laugh. Stuart said, "Okay, I'll admit the guy is a bit brusque until you get to know him, but most workaholic CEO types are. They just get so obsessed with their work, they forget how to communicate with people. Give him a chance, and I'm sure he'll lighten up. I wouldn't have recommended you for the job if I didn't think you two would get along."

"Well, I'm glad you did. I don't have to tell you how desperate I've been to get another job since the last company I worked for had to close. I still can't believe the boss was embezzling. It shocked the crap out of me when the police charged into the place and arrested him. The entire company was unemployed the next day, and I haven't been able to get a job since. It seems like every place I try to apply to already has fifty applicants fighting for the job. Thank goodness I finally got hired someplace, even if it is for the biggest jerk on the planet."

"I don't know why you don't just go into business for yourself. You could make a killing selling that jewelry you're always making." Stuart plucked the bracelet dangling from my wrist for emphasis.

"Thanks, but I need a steady income for things like rent, electricity, and food. I can't just sell jewelry. I'd be homeless in the street in less than three months."

"I told you I didn't mind covering your half of the bills," Stuart insisted.

"I know, but *I* mind. The whole reason I moved here was to be independent. If I wanted someone to take care of me, I'd have just married Mark Hansen like my parents wanted me to."

"Now, there's no need to do something drastic," Stuart teased, making us both laugh.

We ordered pizza delivery for dinner and spent the evening talking and celebrating my new job. Stuart Kline had been my best friend since elementary school, and we loved each other as only the closest friends can. I trusted his judgment about my new boss being a decent guy.

The next morning, my alarm clock failed to go off. Luckily, Stuart got me out of bed in time for my first day of work.

"Damn it! When am I ever going to learn to set the alarm

for a.m. instead of p.m. by accident!" I berated myself as I tumbled out of bed, my left foot catching in the sheets.

"There's no time for that now. Jump in the shower. I'll pick out something for you to wear!" Stuart cried out frantically.

"Thank you! Remember, I need to look like a professional Los Angeles executive assistant for a successful CEO, not some Iowa farm girl," I stated emphatically.

"With your wardrobe, that's going to be hard to pull off," Stuart teased. "Don't you own anything that's not a floral dress? You're not walking in a meadow picking wildflowers, for Pete's sake."

"Just help me pick something!" I shouted out from behind the shower curtain with shampoo running in my eyes.

"Don't worry, sweetie, I bought you a few new things for work with part of my commission check from the beach house. You are going to look model perfect in what I bought you," Stuart stated.

"Stuart!" I cried. "You didn't have to do that!"

I cried tears of gratitude when I saw the new clothes lying on my bed—an entire wardrobe of office-appropriate pencil skirts, blazers, and silk blouses from one of LA's best stores.

"I know, but I wanted to," Stuart said humbly. "You were a true friend to me when I needed it most, and I wanted to return the favor with fashion."

"Thank you, Stuart." I hugged him tight until we both looked at the time and realized I was going to be late for work.

Stuart insisted on helping with my hair and make-up. When he was done, the reflection staring back at me in the mirror was the transformation of my dreams.

Soft make-up that highlighted my violet-gray eyes and pink lips without overpowering them. A classic black pencil skirt that hugged my hips and behind perfectly, with a knee-length hemline that was classy and demure. The lavender silk blouse was feminine and sophisticated, and a pair of low heels that were elegant yet comfortable to walk in all day finished off the ensemble.

It all combined to create the perfect image of professionalism I was going for.

Stuart left my hair down, curling it into soft barrel curls that bounced around my shoulders effortlessly. I accessorized with some of my own jewelry that I'd made myself for fun – a pair of understated, dangling earrings, along with a matching necklace and bracelet. The completed look made me feel beautiful, confident, and sophisticated.

"Stuart, you should quit real estate and become a makeover artist!" I beamed.

"You just go down to that company and show Jack McCann you can handle anything he throws your way," Stuart encouraged.

"I will," I vowed, but inside I wasn't so sure.

Jack McCann ran his company like a tight ship. In our interview, I'd promised him I could handle the job. Now, I prayed that I really could.

Otherwise, all the new wardrobes in the world wouldn't save me from having to take the next bus back to Iowa.

CHAPTER 3

JACK

I woke up before my alarm clock with my heart and mind racing. My dreams had been filled with thoughts of Violet Williams, my sexy new assistant.

I liked her sassy wit, the way she smelled like freshly cut flowers, and her delicious hourglass curves. I had hoped a good night's sleep would get her out of my system. But in my fantasies, just the opposite had happened. Maybe some physical exercise would help clear my mind of these sexual delusions and allow me to treat her with the proper distance I gave all my employees.

I went downstairs to the home gym I'd had installed when I bought the place and quickly put my body through the paces.

Being physically fit had been important to me since the days when my father first started taking out his anger on me when I was a kid. He'd come home from a bad day at work and immediately start drinking. On those nights, it wouldn't be long before he got mean.

Mom always defended him, explaining away his abusive behavior while supplying him with beer. When he started turning his anger on Mom, I knew it was up to me to protect her. I started working out every chance I could until I was strong enough to fight back against him, but I never had the courage.

Then, one night it happened. He turned toward Mom.

I recognized that look in his eyes, and I stepped between them. I punched him with all my seventeen-year-old strength, and he fell to the ground.

I told Mom we needed to move out of the house that night, but she refused to go. He was her husband, she'd said. She still loved him. She even threatened to call the police on *me* for attacking my own father. She always picked him over me, no matter what horrible things he did.

So I left on my own and never looked back. I hadn't spoken to either of them since, but I never forgot that fear of being too weak and small to protect myself. I knew that for the rest of my life, I'd always want to be able to protect myself from those who would hurt me. I had a gym installed at home and worked out every morning and every night.

This morning, I was grateful for it as I poured all my energy into my workout, determined to clear my mind by sweating out the unwanted thoughts.

I ended the workout by running on the treadmill until I was too exhausted to go further. The clock on my wall said I was going to be late for work. Shit! How could I wake up extra early and still be late to the office?

I jumped in the shower to wash off the perspiration, put on a suit, and raced my Porsche to the office.

"It's about time you showed up," Grayson said as I breezed through the door.

I knew I could count on Grayson to bust my balls.

"I guess now that you're LA's 'Sexiest CEO Bachelor,' you're too good for us."

17

"All right, get it out of your system." I rolled my eyes as Grayson bombarded me with bad jokes.

"Did you have trouble picking out what to wear?" he mocked.

"Okay, asshole, you've had your fun. Do you want to joke all day or are you ready to work now?"

In my private office, Grayson and I went over the various details we discussed each day as partners and joint CEOs of our prized company. The problems sparked by Laura's incompetence had been handled, and I let him know a replacement had been hired.

"What's wrong?" Grayson asked, making me realize I was frowning. "You can't be pissed at your new assistant already. She hasn't even started her first day yet."

"It's nothing." I waved my hand as if shooing a fly.

"Don't give me that bullshit. You don't make that face when everything is fine. What's wrong with her?"

"Nothing's wrong with her. In fact, everything is very right with her," I confessed.

Grayson arched an eyebrow. "What does that mean?"

"My new executive assistant just happens to be extremely physically attractive."

"Oh, is she?" Now it was Grayson's turn to frown. "You know we agreed we wouldn't date employees."

"I know, and I have absolutely no intention of asking her out or doing anything even the least bit inappropriate," I vowed solemnly and meant it. "It's just really hard not to notice how smoking hot her body is. That's all."

"Well, find a way not to notice," Grayson suggested. Then he clapped me on the back. "How about I fix you up with that girl I told you about? We can all meet up at the bar after work. I'm telling you, she's good-looking, fun, just your type."

"Forget it. The last time I went out with someone, she turned out to be a real gold digger. In fact, the last three dates I've had were gold diggers. That's why I've sworn off relationships."

"Yeah, keep telling yourself that," Grayson teased. "They say that's when you find love, Mr. Sexiest CEO Bachelor."

"Fuck you." I chuckled with my best friend. "Don't you have work to do, asshole?"

"I sure do. And you do too. It looks like your new EA is here." Grayson nodded his head toward the lobby where Violet had just entered the room. He turned to me and said, "Let me know if you want her to work with me, and you can have my EA instead."

"Thanks, man, but it's okay. I know how to behave like a professional," I assured him. Together, we went to greet Violet.

Impossibly, she looked even more beautiful and sexy than she had during her interview. The way that tight little skirt hugged the curves of her perfectly round ass made my cock twitch.

"This is Violet Williams, our newest hire. I'd like you to meet Grayson, the other CEO of the company." Grayson shook her hand politely. Then he gave me a stern look and retreated to his office, leaving me alone with her. Shit! Suddenly, my mouth went dry, and I couldn't think of what to say. It was like I was twelve years old again, trying to talk to a cute girl for the first time. I was completely tongue-tied.

"Let me show you around the office," I said lamely.

I intended to take her through all the sections of the building, introduce her to the other employees, and make her feel welcome and at home, but something happened to me, and I just couldn't. She was so beautiful and sexy, just standing next to her threatened to give me a massive erection. I didn't want her to see my discomfort, so I refused to move. I was frozen in place like a fucking oak tree. All I could do was just point at things around the office with my arm like a goddamn traffic cop.

"The programmers work right there," I indicated, "and the conference room is down that hall. So is the copy room. The break room is there. That's Grayson's office, and this one is mine."

Violet must have thought I was the worst tour guide in the world, or a complete fucking idiot, as she stood there by my side, bobbing her head along as I pointed at everything.

"Your cubicle is right there, nearest my office. It has everything you need. Make yourself at home. There are some folders on the desk. You're a qualified executive assistant, so I won't waste my time or yours by going over them with you. I'll let you get right to it. The employee handbook will tell you everything you need to know about company procedures and policies. Welcome aboard."

Violet's beautiful violet-gray eyes grew wide, and her mouth was agape. Her lips were so delightfully kissable, it took all my effort not to pull her into my arms and take them. Even her fucking perfume was dangerous, filling my nostrils and putting me under her spell. My cock strained against my slacks, threatening to expose my desire. I had to get out of there. With a curt handshake, I retreated to my office, slammed the door shut, and locked it tight.

Alone at last, I buried my head in my hands and groaned. This was not how I wanted this morning to go.

Shit! I had acted like a complete fucking asshole. It would be a miracle if she didn't quit. I just hoped she wouldn't. After all, it wasn't her fault I was as horny as a teenager. My problem was mine to solve, not hers. I just needed to do what I'd always done when it came to female relationships. I'd wall myself off and focus on business. It was a strategy that had worked flawlessly so far.

But when it came to working with Violet Williams, I could already tell that I'd need a new plan.

CHAPTER 4

VIOLET

*A*lone in my cubicle, I sat and stared at the pile of work Jack McCann had left me with.

No instructions, barely any office orientation, and no introduction to my coworkers. He just pointed to a pile of work, commanded me to do it, and abandoned me to figure out exactly what he wanted me to do completely on my own. How could he demand excellence and perfection without at least providing some instruction?

After reading the employee handbook, I was just as lost as before I'd started. So I turned to my desk and opened the first folder sitting there, but the contents inside were like a foreign language. None of it made any sense to me.

The one thing I knew for sure was that I'd be fired by the end of the week. Maybe even the end of the day, at this rate.

Perhaps my parents were right. Los Angeles was too big a city for an Iowa girl like me. They told me it was a mistake to move so far away from home, hundreds of miles from my family and the town where I'd grown up.

Mark Hansen was a good man, and he'd make a fine and supportive husband. Maybe I was wrong to dismiss him so quickly. So what if I wasn't attracted to him? Maybe I was overreacting when I said I didn't want anyone to support me, that I insisted on pulling my own weight. After all, it turned out that being independent was a lot tougher than I'd thought it would be.

From the moment I'd first moved to LA, life had been one struggle after another. I was just lucky that Stuart was a terrific roommate – not to mention extremely understanding. He never once complained when I was a few days late with my share of the rent or utilities, but paying my fair share was something I wanted to do for myself.

I wanted to be independent and make my own way in the world. I wanted a career and the self-esteem that came with being completely self-reliant. It was why I came to LA in the first place and why I was determined not to be run off by anyone, even a bosshole like Jack McCann.

Suddenly, a head popped up over the top of my cubicle, and a girl with bright blue hair and matching blue frames on her eyeglasses peered down at me.

"How's it going?" she asked. Startled, I nearly fell out of my ergonomic chair. She came around the barrier into my cubicle and thrust her hand out, inviting me to shake it with a friendly smile. "I'm Maddie. Well, Madison Melanie Meecham, but everyone calls me Maddie."

"Your parents named you Madison Melanie Meecham?"

She shrugged. "They had a strange sense of humor."

"Well, it's nice to meet you. I'm Violet." I shook her hand awkwardly.

"I know. Everyone here knows everyone, so when a new face shows up, it's pretty obvious. Lion's like a family that way. It's nicer than my family ever was. How about yours? I assume you're not close with them since you moved here all the way from Iowa. Then again, I could be wrong. Do you want the official tour or what?"

She talked so fast, I was taken aback. It took me a moment to register everything she'd said, and for a second, I just stood there blinking in shock. No one from Iowa talked so fast or so bluntly about personal information.

"How do you know all that about me?" I gaped.

"I'm a programmer for a security company," Maddie said, as if the answer were obvious. Chattering on rapidly, she said, "You'd be amazed at all the information there is about each of us just floating around cyberspace waiting for a nerd like me to find it. Plus, Jack had me do the background check on you before your interview."

"He lets you call him Jack?" I said with surprise. I would have thought the CEO would have insisted all his subordinates called him Mr. McCann like his receptionist had.

"Kate calls everyone by their last name, but the rest of us all go by our first names, even Jack and Grayson. Like I said, Lion is like one big family, but the good kind you want to be a part of and not the kind that drives you crazy. Come on, let me show you around." She grabbed me by the hand and pulled me from my cubicle.

Maddie walked almost as fast as she talked, but I quickly got used to her rapid pace. She introduced me to all the other employees in the office. I knew there was no way I'd remember all their names, but she assured me I would in no time.

"So, what am I supposed to do with all these folders? Is there a list of instructions that I missed or a training guide?" I asked when we returned to my cubicle, and I saw the same pile of folders still stacked ominously on my desk.

"Jack didn't go over these with you?" Maddie shook her blue head with disgust. "You know why cybertech companies keep all their employees in the dark? Because light attracts bugs!"

I didn't get the joke at first, but Maddie snorted and

laughed at her own sense of humor with such obvious delight that I couldn't help but laugh along with her.

"Let me go over how things work with you," Maddie offered kindly. "If I don't know how to do something, I definitely know where to find the information that tells you how."

By the time she was done showing me everything, I felt a lot better about my place in the company. I knew how to perform these tasks, I just hadn't realized that's what Jack wanted. Soon, my fingers were flying over my keyboard as I entered data into spreadsheets.

"After this, do you wanna get a *byte* for lunch?" Maddie offered and then cracked up. "Get it? A byte!"

I laughed along with her. It felt good to have already made a friend.

"Sure," I said and then returned to my work to finish it before lunch break.

She took me to a cute little deli just down the street from Lion, where they had a fantastic vegetarian wrap and the best sweet potato fries in the city, at least according to Maddie.

"These are good, but sometimes I wonder if everyone in California is a vegetarian," I commented around a mouthful of sweet potato fries.

"No, but it can feel that way." Maddie said with an adorable little snort. "So, why did you move away from the Hawkeye State, anyway?"

As we ate lunch, I told her all about my parents' plans to marry me off and my quest to be independent. As my story wrapped up, Maddie suddenly grabbed my hand. "Where did you get this? I absolutely love it!"

"What? Oh, my bracelet. I made it."

"You made this?" Maddie practically ripped it off my wrist so she could study it more closely. "This craftsmanship is amazing. You have a true talent. Have you designed any other jewelry?"

"Actually, I have," I said, feeling my face turn warm. "Making jewelry has been a hobby of mine since I was a kid. I used to fantasize about owning my own jewelry store someday, but as I got older, I realized how ridiculous that was."

"I don't think so. This heart design is fantastic! Have you sold many of these?" Maddie put the bracelet on her wrist and watched as the heart sparkled in the sunlight.

"Oh, no. I just make them for friends and for something fun to do." I flushed bright pink. "It's how I unwind after a stressful day."

"Well, *would* you ever sell one?" Maddie pressed. I felt my stomach flutter. Nobody had ever asked me that before, but it had been a fantasy of mine for years before I realized what a pipe dream it was.

The odds of making it as a successful jewelry designer were tiny. If I wanted to be independent, I needed a practical career that I could actually make a living at. It was why I went to business school and took my job so seriously.

Still, to have someone tell me they liked my jewelry so much they wanted to buy it made my heart soar.

Maddie returned the bracelet to me, and I fumbled trying to put it back on. Still flushing, I said, "I don't know. I've never thought about selling my jewelry. I guess I would if anybody was interested in buying it, but who would want to give me money for something like this?"

"I would," Maddie insisted. "Do you think you could make me a bracelet just like this one with the pi symbol on it instead of a heart? I'd pay you good money for it."

"I'm sure I could," I said brightly. I'd made a pendant in the shape of the popular math symbol for a math teacher once as a gift. It wasn't that complicated, and I was certain I still had the pattern. It would be a pleasure to make one for Maddie. "But you don't need to pay me for it."

"Don't be ridiculous. Your jewelry is much too valuable for you just to be giving it away like it's worthless. Think of the cost of the supplies and your skills and creativity, not to mention your time and effort. Now add it all up and tell me, what would you charge for a bracelet like that?"

I thought carefully and named a price. Maddie scoffed and told me to double it.

"Are you sure you want to pay that much?" I couldn't believe it.

"Don't doubt your own worth," Maddie insisted. "Besides, once the other programmers in the office see me wearing it, they'll all want one, and then you'll be working night and day making them. So, you'd better set the price right in the beginning, or you're screwed."

I thought about what Maddie said about knowing my own self-worth. When we returned to the office after lunch, I decided to do the very best job I could for Jack McCann. By showing him the true value and worth of what I could bring to the company, I was certain I could gain his respect.

By the end of the work day, my pulse was racing as I turned in the completed files to Jack. I held my head up high. I wouldn't let him see how nervous I was.

He looked them over slowly and then turned his gaze to meet mine. His deep blue eyes drew me in, and I felt the tiny hairs on my arms stand up. Then, the corners of his lips curved into the barest of smiles. It was almost imperceptible, but I caught it, and it made me light up inside.

"You did good work today. Go ahead and call it a day. I'll see you tomorrow morning."

I WAS PRACTICALLY SKIPPING as I entered my apartment to find Stuart cooking dinner with his current boyfriend, Andy.

"There's our industrious little Midwestern girl!" Andy exclaimed, looking up from the saucepan he was stirring.

"So, how was your first day on the job?" Stuart asked before I'd even taken off my jacket. Clearly, he was dying of curiosity. I decided to have a little fun with him.

"Terrible and wonderful," I said cryptically.

"Terrible how?" Stuart prodded.

"Your real estate client Jack McCann is a complete boss-hole. He's in love with his company, but he couldn't spare two minutes to talk to me. I don't know how I'm going to tolerate working with him."

"I'm sorry, sweetie." Stuart gave me a brotherly hug.

"However, I did make a terrific new friend today," I said, turning my attention to the bright side of my day. "Her name is Maddie, and she showed me the good things about working at this company. All the employees at Lion are really nice, except for Jack, and I really enjoyed the work. It's satisfying to use the skills I learned in business school."

"That's great, Violet. But are you sure you want to work for a company where the boss is an asshole to you?" Stuart asked cautiously.

I thought about it carefully, and the more I did, the more certain I was.

"Absolutely," I said. "I'm going to show the world what I'm capable of. I've finally found my independence, and there's no way I'm giving it up. No one's going to stop me. Not even a jerk like Jack McCann."

CHAPTER 5

JACK

"*H*ere are this week's reports," Violet said as she handed me a stack of papers.

I leafed through them. She'd been working for me for nearly two weeks, and she did excellent work, but I still wanted to review things out of an abundance of caution.

"Everything looks good." I flashed her a smile, but then I caught myself in the act, and I didn't want to appear like I was flirting with her.

Shit! Why was I so damn attracted to Violet Williams?

I'd worked with plenty of gorgeous women in the past, and none of them had this prolonged effect on me. In fact, no woman had ever made me feel the way I did about Violet. She haunted my dreams and even my waking hours too. I found myself thinking about her when I should have been concentrating on work.

I was the CEO of a successful company, and I had a schoolboy crush on my assistant. Not only did it cut into my productivity, but I sure as hell didn't want the other employees to catch on.

There was only one solution. I'd have to fortify the wall I'd built around my heart.

The wall went up the day I had to leave my family to save myself, and I'd just kept adding bricks to it every day since. It was the reason I'd never had a serious relationship or even been in love. It was the reason I ran a top security company worth millions of dollars. Yes, walling off my heart was the best solution to keeping Violet out of my thoughts. I had to focus on my company – the one thing in life that had never hurt me.

I wiped the annoying smile off my face and looked at Violet. "Let's go over the areas where these files show the company needs improvement."

Violet pulled up a chair and sat next to me at my desk. As we passed the reports back and forth discussing them, just for an instant, our hands touched. Her skin was so soft, and she always smelled so good, like a garden of flowers. I wanted to run my hands through her thick mane of chestnut curls and caress her cheek.

I snatched the papers away from her to break the spell. "That's enough," I snapped. "I've got a lot of work to do. Close the door on your way out."

"Certainly. If it's all right, I thought I'd take my lunch break now," she said, apparently unfazed by my brusque demeanor.

I longed to hold her close and tell her I was sorry I was such a jerk, but I told the sentimental part of myself to fuck right off.

"Fine," I said dismissively, staring intently at the papers to avoid her gaze.

Violet left, and I felt like shit for the way I'd treated her. She was an excellent assistant. In fact, she deserved my constant praise. Violet was practical, efficient, and hard-working. The company had been thriving ever since she came on board.

I put in long days, but she was always the first person to arrive in the office and never left at the end of the night until I dismissed her, sometimes hours after everyone else had gone home. And not once did she ever complain. I was truly impressed by her work ethic, but I could never tell her for fear she'd see how much I liked her.

I poured myself into my job night and day, determined to block out my feelings for Violet. If anyone found out I was attracted to an employee, the scandal could ruin my company, and I absolutely couldn't let that happen.

The business was my baby, the culmination of a lifetime of hard work. This business had saved me when I was young, hiding in my best friend's garage to develop a system that would protect people from predators. Lion gave me a sense of purpose. It made others respect me and taught me to have confidence in myself.

It had pulled me out of poverty. The lifestyle I grew up with – barely getting by each month, standing in lines at the food bank – was long gone. I no longer lived in fear of ending up homeless. I could even give back to the food banks and resources that had helped me during those times when Dad had spent all our grocery money buying beer.

Plus, I'd created a scholarship specifically for under-privileged youth interested in the computer sciences. Then, I gave those scholarship recipients jobs once they gradu-ated. Maddie had been one of the first recipients of the Lion Scholarship, and many more had followed. Some had stayed with Lion, but others had gone on to do great things of their own, and it filled me with pride. I'd never have been able to lift up other poor kids like me if it hadn't been for the success of the company I'd built with Grayson.

I had brought Lion into existence and given the company

life. In return, it had given me a better life than I ever could have imagined for myself.

I wasn't about to risk my company for some woman I just happened to have a crush on, no matter how utterly amazing she was.

Pushing her from my mind, I headed over to a cluster of programmers to run an idea past them. I was deep in conversation when Violet returned from lunch, chatting happily to the receptionist as she entered the lobby.

Hearing her laugh and seeing her smile as she walked into the room made me stop mid-sentence. My heart skipped a beat. The way the sunlight fell on her hair was mesmerizing, and I completely lost my train of thought.

The programmers were staring at me, waiting for me to finish what I was saying. I struggled to regain my composure. Violet had stolen my heart once more, only this time there had been an audience to see it happen. Shit! Everyone in that room could see right through me. I had to do something to keep myself from being exposed for liking Violet.

"It's about time you showed up to work," I called across the room, making Violet freeze. I gave her an icy look. "Lunch is one hour long, not an hour and ten minutes."

"My apologies. It won't happen again," she said, turning to look back at me.

Violet held her head high, meeting my gaze as if to say she would not be intimidated.

"Make certain it doesn't. Employees are expected to be at work at their scheduled time. Any deviation is unacceptable," I stated firmly. I knew I sounded like a dick, but I couldn't let my employees think I was showing favoritism toward her, even if it made me look like a complete asshole.

"Well, that's clearly not true." Violet crossed her arms over her chest as her violet-gray eyes flashed. "I've been arriving at work fifteen minutes early every day, and you've never once complained about that."

My eyes narrowed. "Make a company-wide memo informing all employees of a new policy," I stated furiously, trying to regain some sense of authority in the room. Inside, though, I was applauding her for calling me out on my own hypocritical bullshit. She was fearless as well as brilliant. "From now on, no employee will arrive to work early or late without my direct authorization or approval. Is that clear?"

"Perfectly," Violet said, her eyes fiery. She retreated to her cubicle as the rest of the employees scattered. Grayson followed me into my office.

"What the fuck was that all about?" Grayson asked the moment the door shut behind him. "You've never cared about that kind of corporate bullshit before. You're losing your fucking mind. You need to get out of the office and have some fun before you blow a fuse."

"Maybe you're right." I ran a hand through my hair with a heavy sigh.

Grayson gripped my shoulder. "You're going out tonight, and I won't accept any of your excuses. It's been way too long since we hit the bar."

"Thanks, but I'm not quite in the mood," I said, but Grayson refused to be brushed off so easily. We'd been friends for too long. He knew me too well.

"That's exactly why you need to go out. Remember, you asked me to let you know when you're becoming a workaholic ass. Guess what? You're there."

I realized Grayson was right. I was taking my own personal issues out on Violet – and all my other employees too.

That night, I went home to shower and change, then I met Grayson down at the bar.

It was a Friday night in LA, and the place was packed. But

the bouncer recognized me and Grayson and let us in right away. I paid for a private booth, and Grayson ordered a bottle of their best scotch. It felt good as it went down smooth, and I closed my eyes, savoring the sensation as it warmed through my body, washing away my stresses.

"Hey, Ashley!" Grayson saw a sexy blonde across the bar and waved her over. "This is my buddy I wanted you to meet, Jack McCann. Jack, this is Ashley Stokes. Her sister bartends here. We got to talking one night, and I figured you two would hit it off."

"Pleased to meet you." Ashley stuck out a manicured hand, and I shook it.

"I'm going to give you some privacy so you two can get to know each other," Grayson said as he slipped out of the booth.

"No, wait!" I tried to stop him, but it was too late. Grayson had escaped to talk to a voluptuous redhead, and Ashley quickly took his place, sliding into the booth next to me with catlike reflexes.

I sighed. "So, tell me about yourself," I said uncomfortably.

She was pretty enough but not quite my type, with bleached blonde hair, enhanced breasts, and bright pink lipstick to match her inch-long nails. Her clothes were too tight, and her heels were too high. Nothing about her seemed authentic. Not even her laugh, as it boomed over the sound of the music and the crowd.

Ashley was nothing like Violet, with her country wholesomeness and her sincere smile. Violet had a purity of spirit that was irreproachable, even when she was giving me sass. It was one of things I liked most about her, how she used honesty and humor to hold everyone accountable, including me, and most especially herself. I knew I could trust her. This blonde was the complete opposite of Violet, fake and plastic. She had gold digger written all over her.

"You know, I'm feeling tired and I've got a big meeting at work early in the morning." I tried to excuse myself, but she was quicker than I would have given her credit for.

"I'm tired too. Can you give me a ride home?" She batted her big blue eyes at me as her hands wrapped around my arm, and there was no way I could say no.

"Sure," I said glumly. I stood, and she latched onto me, keeping pace with me as I walked. Grayson gave me a thumbs-up as we passed by. Outside, I waved over a taxi and held the door open for Ashley.

"Aren't you a true gentleman?" Ashley grinned as she climbed into the car, and I gently closed her door. Then, I reached into the front window of the cab and handed the driver a hundred-dollar bill.

"Take her home, please," I said.

Ashley's smile instantly disappeared as she started screaming obscenities at me. "What the fuck! I thought you were coming home with me! You asshole!"

I had to stifle a laugh as the cab drove away and her voice faded into the distance. It was a cruel trick, but there was no way I was letting her follow me home.

The valet brought out my Porsche, and I enjoyed the feel of the wind in my face as I sped through the city streets and down the long canyon road leading up to my house overlooking the ocean. It was the beach house I'd just purchased from that realtor who had recommended Violet, and it was my perfect oasis. I loved going there to escape from the stress of the office. It was the one place I never brought work with me and the one place where I could truly unwind. Maybe there I could finally escape my thoughts of Violet. Obviously, nothing else I'd tried had worked.

I poured a glass of fine scotch over ice, flicked on some music, and fell onto the couch.

My hands slid down the waistband of my slacks, and my thoughts turned unbidden to Violet. The way her skin had been so soft when we touched hands at work. The brush of her breast on my arm as she reached past me to grab a pencil. The sway of those curved hips as she walked through the room. That perfectly round ass as she bent to pick up a piece of paper she'd dropped.

Soon my hand was stroking my rock-hard dick, faster and faster. I pictured her face, those violet eyes, those kissable soft pink lips.

Oh, Violet, how I've longed to fuck you.

Fuck! I exploded in orgasm into a hand towel, breathless, my heart racing. Maybe jerking off was what I needed to release the desire I felt for Violet.

But somehow, I doubted anything short of having her would ever be enough.

CHAPTER 6

VIOLET

"*I*'m so glad today is finally over," I groaned as I collapsed onto the couch after coming home from work.

As usual, Stuart was home from his office before me. Not only did he make triple my income, he worked fewer hours too.

"Tough day, sweetie?" Stuart breezed into the kitchen to pour me a margarita from the fridge. He handed it to me.

"My boss, that jerk Jack McCann, was riding me all day."

"I wouldn't mind him riding *me* all day," Stuart quipped, but I ignored him.

Taking the margarita gratefully, I took a large sip and said, "He's just such an ass, nitpicking over every little detail. I was ten minutes late coming back from lunch, and he pounced on me in front of the whole company, but I got back at him. Ugh, he's such a bosshole!"

"Maybe you could use a good pouncing of a completely different type," Stuart said, and I just rolled my eyes at the innuendo.

"Forget it," I said with an edge of hostility.

"I'm serious," Stuart insisted. "When was the last time you got laid? I don't think I've seen you with anybody since you dumped loser Nathan. You deserve some happiness. Want me to set you up with somebody? I know some straight guys who'd be perfect for you."

"Hmm. You also said working for Jack the Jerk McCann would be perfect for me. No thanks. He is such a… a jerk!" I said, unable to think of a better word.

My margarita glass was soon empty, and I went to the kitchen to refill it, picking up Stuart's empty glass on the way.

"How was your day?" I asked with a sigh.

"Oh, you know, living the dream," he said with a wave of his hand. "There's another beach property coming up, and Carol says I can sell it. I'm going to be rolling in the dough soon, Vi. God, I love my job!"

I narrowed my eyes and shot him a glare.

He cringed. "Sorry!"

"Rub it in some more, Stuey. You have the perfect job, and I have to work for a total sadist."

Stuart looked me up and down with a knowing smile. "Sweetie, you sure do talk about Jack an awful lot."

"He's my boss. I'm stuck working with every day. He thinks he's so smart, handsome, and sexy. You should see the way he takes off his tailored jacket. I can see his rippling biceps through his designer shirts. And that smile of his and those penetrating eyes. Jack McCann is full of himself, but he's really just a… just a…"

"Let me guess, a jerk?" Stuart mocked. "Listen sweetie, I've known you long enough to recognize when you're crushing on someone, and you've got it for your boss, bad."

"I do not! That's ridiculous!" I cried out, feeling utterly aghast. "Just because he's confident, and witty, and smells incredible, doesn't mean I like him. You *know* he's not my type."

"Intelligent, wealthy, charismatic? Oh, no. Of course not. Why would you want any of that in a man? Especially after your last boyfriend couldn't even hold down a job and needed you to buy his groceries."

"Shut up!" I threw a dishtowel at Stuart, hitting him right in the face, and we both laughed. I looked down at the countertop and saw that the towel had been covering a pile of mail with my name on it.

"What's this?" I picked up the first letter in the stack. It was a credit card bill for a motorcycle I'd never purchased. The next letter was another credit card bill, and so was the next and the next.

Horrified, I pored over all the collection notices. They were all for credit cards in my name but used at stores that I didn't shop at, for items that I never bought. A leather jacket, a motorcycle helmet, cowboy boots, tons of pizza?

"What the hell?" Stuart asked, glancing at the letters. "None of these purchases are yours."

My pulse quickened, and I could feel my face getting hot.

"You know who this sounds like?" I looked at Stuart, and he nodded in agreement.

My blood was boiling as I dialed Nathan's number. To my surprise, he actually answered.

"Did you take my credit cards when I broke up with you?" I shouted into the phone. I meant to start more diplomatically, but I was so mad, I couldn't stop the words.

"No, you left them at my place in that wallet you said was for emergencies. I figured it was a gift," he said. I could picture his smirk.

"So you decided to use them for a shopping spree? You selfish son of a bitch!"

"Easy with the name-calling. You always said I should be more responsible. I was just taking care of some necessities that I needed in order to grow up and be a man. Weren't those your exact words to me just before you left me the cards?"

"I did not authorize you to use those, and you know it! I'll call the cops. I'll press fraud charges, Nathan. You're going to have to pay me back every cent you put on those cards."

"Good luck with that," Nathan scoffed. The sound of his idiotic guffaw made me sick to my stomach. "I don't have a job or any assets, or even a bank account. You can sue me all you want, but you'll never get a dime out of me. There's always another gullible girl out there willing to take care of me. All I have to do is tell her what she wants to hear."

"I can't believe you! We dated for months. You're really going to stick me with this mountain of debt you accumulated? Even *you* can't be that big of a dick!"

"Once again, you underestimate me." Nathan laughed cruelly and hung up.

My eyes locked with Stuart, who gazed at me sympathetically.

"I'm screwed," I whispered.

I WAS STILL FUMING about it the next day at work. There was no way around it. I'd be stuck paying for Nathan's shopping spree.

And it wasn't just the matter of the bills. I was kicking myself for my own bad judgment in men.

How could I ever have fallen for Nathan – that worthless, selfish, lazy piece of crap? Well, never again!

I wanted a man with integrity and ambition, one who knew how to work hard and took pride in a job well done. A man who was successful but not arrogant or greedy, a man like…

Without realizing it, my gaze turned to Jack McCann's office door.

No, not him. *Definitely* not him.

Sure, he was the sexiest, handsomest man I'd ever seen. Everything about him oozed charisma, from his tailored suits to his charming grin. I'd even caught him staring at me a few times with a far-off look in his dreamy eyes, as if he were attracted to me. But that was ridiculous.

What would a millionaire hunk like Jack McCann ever see in a simple Iowa girl like me? If anything, he was probably thinking about his beloved company. Jack cared more about Lion than anything. He was an absolute workaholic. Every morning, I tried to come in earlier than he did just to show him up, and I never succeeded. He probably got to work before dawn.

It was easy to see how much Jack loved his company, and even his employees. It surprised me to learn how very generous he was. Maddie herself told me how he mentored her, put her through college, and then gave her a job after she graduated.

"I thought maybe he was going to be one of those creeps who would lord it over me for personal favors, but he's only treated me with respect," Maddie confided.

"So why is he always so rude to me?" I wondered aloud, making Maddie shrug.

"He's got a brilliant mind," Maddie offered. "He's always thinking of better ways to keep his clients secure and improve the business. Sometimes when he gets like that, he goes off into his own little world and snaps at people. Don't take it personally or as an insult. He's told me himself many times that you're an excellent assistant and he's happy he hired you."

"Well, he sure doesn't show it," I said.

"That's just his way. He doesn't show much of himself. He keeps it all hidden. You'd never know he donated all his profits last month to a domestic violence shelter. I saw the check. A lot of CEOs use charities for a tax write-off or to get good publicity, but Jack insisted the shelter keep his donation anonymous."

"Hmm."

I was more impressed than I wanted to admit, and more than a little confused about what kind of man Jack McCann truly was.

At the end of the day, I knocked quietly on his office door to turn in my files to him. When he didn't respond, I cautiously opened the door. After all, I knew he was in there.

To my surprise, he was dancing around the office, singing the lyrics of a cheesy classic rock song – "Rock You Like a Hurricane." He actually wasn't half bad at dancing, though his voice was totally off-key. Unable to stifle my laughter, I giggled into my hands, and he looked up at me, startled.

"Sorry to interrupt," I said, hiding my grin behind my files. "I knocked, but I guess you didn't hear me. Is that... the Scorpions?"

"Yeah, sorry about that." Jack turned off the music and shoved his hands in his pockets awkwardly. "I was just unwinding after a long day, letting off some steam."

"It's okay, I get it," I said. It was kind of adorable seeing him looking like a shy kid caught dancing in his room. His look of chagrin was even sexier than his confident smile, and I felt drawn to comfort him. Setting the files on his desk, I touched his hand gently and said, "I've had a rough time lately, too."

I'd been thinking of my problems with Nathan, not antic-ipating that Jack might take it another way.

"Yeah, I owe you an apology for that too." Jack clasped his other hand on top of mine so that my hand was sandwiched between both of his in a supportive clasp. "I know I come across pretty harsh sometimes. I just want you to know you're doing really great work here. I appreciate it far more than I ever say."

"Thank you. I appreciate that." I flushed. My heart was beating so fast, I could feel my pulse rushing through my veins. As Jack kept holding my hand, I stepped closer to him, our eyes locked, my palms sweating.

Suddenly, the phone rang on Jack's desk, startling us both and causing us to break apart.

"I've got to take this call," Jack said urgently, his forehead beading with sweat.

"Yeah, I was just checking to see if I could go home for the night or if you needed me to stay."

"No, no. Go home. I'll see you tomorrow." Jack flushed, and my cheeks were burning bright red as I left his office. Thank goodness everyone else had already left for the day so that no one could see what an effect he'd had on me when he held my hand and gazed into my eyes. It was like all the rest of the world had disappeared and we alone were destined to be together.

I couldn't stop thinking about it on the drive home. Once I arrived at the apartment, I found a note on the counter from Stuart. He was out with Andy and wouldn't be back until the morning. He'd saved me some leftovers in the fridge for dinner, but I wasn't hungry yet. I just poured myself a glass of wine and decided to take a hot bath. Between work and Nathan, and now my brief sensuous moment with Jack, I needed to unwind.

I poured some lavender oil in the tub, lit some candles, and sipped my wine while the steaming hot water filled the basin. I turned on some music, and for fun, I picked an old

'80s rock ballad just to be silly. As the guitar solo soared, I could see why this kind of music appealed to Jack.

I sank down into the tub and let the hot water melt my tension. It was pure heaven, and I luxuriated in it, only my mind kept drifting to thoughts of Jack. His unguarded smile, his sparkling eyes, the way it felt when his hand was holding mine. Hearing him say how much he appreciated me and seeing the look in his face when he was truly vulnerable.

My hands slid down my naked body and found the triangle of my sex. I closed my eyes and thought of Jack as I rubbed my delicate folds, imagining his big, rough hands there instead. I knew he'd look amazing underneath that suit, with his muscled body hovering above me. And best of all, his thick, hard cock, plunging into my depths.

The thought of Jack filling me up, thrusting inside me, pushed me over the edge. My body tingled as I brought myself to the apex of pleasure in a way I hadn't done in a long time. I gasped as my body shuddered, riding the waves of the climax.

I came down from the orgasm, suddenly aware of what I'd just done.

I'd fantasized about Jack McCann.

What did it all mean? Was I attracted to Bosshole Supreme? Was Stuart right and all the hatred I felt toward Jack was really just my desire to jump into bed with him?

No, it couldn't be.

But as I plunged deeper into the warm water, there was no use denying that I was attracted to Jack.

Despite his kind words that afternoon, he'd still humiliated me in front of my coworkers. And he'd made the first days of my job hellish.

But that didn't matter.

Because I wanted Jack McCann more than I'd ever wanted any man.

CHAPTER 7

I stood in the shower for a long time, letting the steaming hot water pour over my aching muscles. I'd spent the night dreaming about Violet. No matter how hard I tried, I just couldn't get her out of my mind. I'd never felt this way about a woman before, and the fact that she was forbidden fruit only made it worse.

Unable to sleep past dawn, I gave up tossing and turning in bed. I got up to hit the gym hard. Then, I took an extra hot shower, trying to wash away my obsession with Violet along with all the sweat. It didn't work. Nothing worked.

She was gorgeous, no doubt about it. But more than that, I enjoyed her sense of humor, her intelligence, and her wit. Every day she made me smile, and I had a reason other than my work addiction to look forward to going to the office now.

As I turned off the shower, I heard the sound of my cell phone ringing in the master bedroom. Shit!

Wrapping a towel around my waist, I rushed to my night-stand and picked it up. The screen said Unknown Caller. I was extremely careful about who I gave my personal cell phone number to, so it had to be someone I knew, but when I answered I didn't recognize the person on the other end of the line.

"Hey, baby," a strange female voice crooned. "I've decided to forgive you for the misunderstanding we had last night. You can make it up to me by coming over to my place tonight for dinner."

"Who is this?" I blanked.

She forced a laugh. "You're so funny, Jack. We weren't so drunk last night that you don't remember me."

"Ashley Stokes, from the bar last night." It suddenly dawned on me who she was. "How did you get this phone number?"

"Grayson Lewis gave it to me," she said, trying to sound sexy.

"Great, I'll have to thank him for that."

"Me too." Ashley missed my sarcasm. "I'm so glad he introduced us. I felt a real connection between us. So, what time should I expect you for dinner?"

"Listen, Ashley. I appreciate the invitation, but –" I was about to tell her we couldn't see each other again when she cut me off with a rush of words.

"You know, dinner's so far away. I don't want to wait that long to see you. I'm going to be near your office building this afternoon. What are you doing for lunch today? We could meet up then."

She sounded so hopeful. I hated to hurt her feelings, but odds were she was just looking to cash in on a juicy, falsified story of how I'd slept with her and didn't call back. Or maybe she'd say that I broke her heart over lunch. Then her lawyer would contact my office and ask for a payoff to bury the story. Well, she could forget it. I'd been around enough gold diggers to recognize one a mile away, and I wasn't falling for her scam.

"No. I can't meet you for lunch or dinner. In fact, I think it's better if we don't plan on seeing each other again," I said gently yet firmly. You could never tell when a woman was recording a phone conversation, and I didn't want to sound too willing or too callous. It was an impossible line to walk.

"I agree," Ashley said with a surprising amount of cheer. "It's a lot more fun if we just surprise each other!"

"No, Ashley. You misunderstood. We're not right for each other," I tried to say, but I kept getting interrupted with another incoming call. "Listen, Ashley, I have to take this call coming in."

"Okay, I'll talk to you later. I'll surprise you sometime," Ashley said. She hung up before I could tell her not to.

"No. Don't do that. Ah, shit!" I muttered aloud.

"You don't even know what I'm calling about, and you're already turning me down," the other caller said, and this time I recognized the voice right away.

"Jerome!" I cried out happily. "Sorry, I was talking to a woman on the other line, telling her not to....ah, never mind. It's too long a story."

"No need to explain. I know what dating is like these days," Jerome said with an easy chuckle. He was a long-time business associate and one of my very first customers. We'd known each other since before Lion even had an office building.

"What are you calling for at this early hour?" I asked him with the easy banter of good friends.

"Vista Hotels," Jerome said simply.

"Thanks, but I don't want to go away with you to a hotel," I joked.

"You will after this," Jerome replied with deadpan humor. "An inside source told me Howard Morris, owner of Vista Hotels, is looking for a new cybersecurity company. Nobody

47

knows yet. It could be a golden opportunity for you and Lion, Inc."

"Are you fucking serious?" My mouth was already watering. "That chain must have over a hundred hotels in California alone, let alone across the country."

I listened as Jerome told me everything he knew about Howard Morris and his massive national hotel chain. The more he said, the more I wanted that account. Having a client like that would be a huge bolster to Lion, and it could lead to doing cybersecurity for even more hotel chains for the company.

"Thanks, man," I said. "I owe you big for this one."

"Just give my business free service and we'll call it even," Jerome joked, knowing full well that I already did.

We hung up and I rushed to get dressed, forgetting my tie in the process, but I didn't care. I had to get to the office to talk to Grayson about this right away.

Grayson was just as excited as I had been. "This opportunity is fantastic, and it couldn't have come at a better time. Our books are in serious trouble right now and we desperately need the boost."

"We're not in the red yet," I said defensively.

"No, but after the issues we had last quarter because of that awful assistant Laura, we can't afford to be donating to all your big philanthropic causes coming up soon, and if I know you, you'll give to them anyway."

"I give to those charities out of my share of the profits. It doesn't hurt the company," I pointed out.

"Yeah, but I donate my profits back into the company, so by you not doing the same, it does hurt us. I know you grew up poor and it really sucked, but it's not up to you to save the whole rest of the world. We have a duty to our employees and our clients. We can't keep doing right by them without reinvesting our profits, unless we get more profits coming in."

"Enough. We can debate this later. Right now, we have a chance to pitch to Morris and Vista Hotels before anyone else even knows he's fucking looking. I want to land this account before word gets out and the competition gets fierce. We need to get started right away."

"Agreed," Grayson said and we gave each other a high-five just like we used to do back in his garage.

We spent the entire morning holed up in my office trying to come up with a winning concept to pitch to Morris, but the task turned out to be a lot tougher than I thought it would be.

We could have handed it down for our sales crew to handle, but with a client as big and important as Howard Morris, I felt it was important for the sales pitch to come directly from me and Grayson. After all, the fate of our company might be riding on it. I'd looked at the books, and Grayson was right. If we didn't get more income soon, I would have to cut back on my charitable donations or reduce my staff, and I wanted to avoid doing both at all costs.

As the morning drew on, however, I remembered just how bad I was at selling. I was much more talented at the tech side of business than the selling side, which tended to make me feel cheesy. Grayson was just as bad at it, and the two of us took turns shooting down each other's horrible ideas until our heads hurt.

"This isn't working," Grayson groaned.

"I think we're getting worse." I leaned my head forward and let it bang painfully against my desk.

Suddenly a soft knock came at my door and Violet entered the room wearing a pale pink skirt that showed off her shapely legs and a soft pink sweater to match. Her chestnut hair was pulled back into a ponytail with soft tendrils framing her beautiful face. She was a vision of sweet loveliness, and for a moment, all my frustrations were gone.

"I thought you two must be hungry," Violet said as she set down a tray of sandwiches on my desk. I looked at my watch and was surprised to see it was already mid-afternoon and we had worked right through lunch.

"Thanks." Grayson eagerly reached for a sandwich and took a big bite. As he swallowed, he said to Violet, "I was starving. Jack always says it's your terrific intuition that makes you such a great EA."

"He does?" Violet blushed at the compliment. I wanted to shove that sandwich all the way into Grayson's mouth to stop him from talking. I'd told him that about Violet in complete confidence, not so he could tell the woman I had a crush on that I admired her.

To cover, I said awkwardly, "We've got a lot of work to do here. So please shut the door on your way out."

I hated to sound dismissive, but I couldn't have her standing there looking so sexy, watching me while I dripped mustard down my shirt.

"Of course," Violet said, and moved towards the door. Fuck, she looked even more sensuous leaving than she did when she was standing next to me. I could never get tired of watching those hips move when she walked away.

She was just about to close the door when suddenly Violet turned back once more. "By the way, I've collected some personal data on the Morris family in case you needed it. I can bring you the file if you'd like."

"What made you do that?" I asked, again sounded like a dickhead. What was wrong with me? Why couldn't I sound like a normal guy whenever I talked to Violet?

Violet said, "Well, you've been asking me for a lot of data on Howard Morris and his chain of hotels all morning, so I figured you might like some information on his family too."

"It's not your job to second-guess what I need," I chastised. Shit, now she must think I was the biggest asshole on the planet. Maybe it was for the best. At least this way she'd never know just how much I liked her.

Violet was unflappable as always. Instead of flipping me off like I deserved, she just smiled and said, "Lucky for you, I provide that service for free."

She handed me the file, and I was impressed by the amount of information she had gathered, but I was afraid I didn't quite see the point.

"What's all this useless information for?" I asked, glancing at the pages.

"Well, if you read all these articles, you'll see there's a common element to all of his interviews. Mr. Morris always says that the most important factor in his life isn't his hotel chain, it's his family. No matter what he's doing or where he's going, he's always thinking of his family and wanting to put their safety and well-being first."

"What are you getting at?" I wanted to be sure I understood what I thought she meant.

"If you want to catch Mr. Morris's interest, all you have to do is show him how Lion, Inc., cybersecurity won't just help protect his business, it will protect his family too," Violet beamed.

"You know, that sounds pretty fucking good," Grayson said, and I had to agree.

"It does," I said, smiling right at Violet. "And since you thought of it, I'm going to need you to work extra hours all this week helping us turn your idea into the perfect sales pitch for Morris."

CHAPTER 8

VIOLET

"The sales pitch is good, but if we just make this little change here, it becomes even better," I said, underlining a section of text on the document.

"Don't move that," Jack started to say, but then he froze mid-sentence and his scowl transformed into a smile. "That's better. Let's make those same changes over here."

"You got it, boss," I said with a smile.

Working side by side with Jack on the pitch to Howard Morris and Vista Hotels was simultaneously exhausting and exhilarating. The hours were grueling, but I didn't mind. After all, I could use the extra money to pay down some of the debt Nathan had dumped on me.

If I was being completely honest, I enjoyed spending so much alone time with Jack.

The truth was that the impossible had happened – I'd grown to actually *like* Jack McCann.

Over the past few weeks, I'd come to realize he wasn't actually the jerk I thought he was. He lived and breathed for the cybersecurity company he'd built from nothing, and it occupied his head space. So a lot of the times his brusqueness meant he was simply lost in thought or focused on his company.

In those moments, I'd discovered a trick. All I had to do was turn on a little classic rock music in his office, and he calmed right down. There was something about the beat and the guitar solos that lifted away his stress and made him want to dance instead. Once, he even grabbed me by the hand and asked me to dance with him.

"I don't know how to dance to this kind of music," I'd confessed with a blush as his touch sent thrills shooting through me.

"Nonsense. Everybody can dance to this. You just relax your body and let the beat carry you away."

I'd never laughed so hard or had so much fun.

Unfortunately, there was no time for dancing today. The deadline was looming over us with a meeting scheduled with Howard Morris himself at Jack's favorite bar tomorrow night, and our presentation for the sales pitch had to be perfect by then.

"Remove that part. It's too sentimental," Jack criticized, but I refused to let him push my opinion aside.

"You should keep it just the way that it is. Focusing on how cybersecurity affects the families of those it protects will really resonate with Mr. Morris. Trust me."

Jack was silent, and when I looked up to see if he was pissed off at me for arguing with him, I was surprised to see him staring at me with a passionate look brewing in his deep blue eyes.

"I do trust you," he said softly.

Then, he leaned in toward me slowly, as if to kiss me.

I could hardly believe it. I'd longed for this moment for so long, and suddenly it was happening. Holding my breath in anticipation, I moistened my lips and awaited his embrace.

Then, Jack leaned past me, reaching across the desk for his calculator that was on the other side of me.

"Excuse me," he mumbled absentmindedly as he grabbed it and then straightened.

I felt like such a fool. My entire face was flushed with embarrassment, but the worst part was realizing how disappointed I was.

Stuart had been right. I did have a crush on Jack. I could finally admit it to myself. But that didn't help with the pain of knowing my feelings weren't mutual.

I'd wanted him to kiss me since the first moment I saw him. Of course, it was impossible, but thinking for just that brief moment he might actually want me too filled me with an indescribable hope.

Then, that hope was smashed into pieces.

"Are you all right?" Jack suddenly put his hands on my shoulders and gazed at me with a worried expression.

I liked the way it felt to have him holding me like that, but I knew better than to fall for the same illusion twice. Jack didn't have any romantic feelings for me like I did for him. The moments I'd thought he might have wanted to kiss me were caused by my imagination running away from me. None of it was real, and hoping otherwise would only cause me heartache.

Shaking my head, I said, "I'm fine. It's just been a long day, and I haven't eaten anything since breakfast."

"I guess we did work through lunch. Now it's getting late." Jack was startled by the time as he looked at his watch. "Let's take a break, and I'll buy you dinner at my favorite eatery."

"You don't have to do that. I'm not that hungry." I waved him off, but then my stomach rumbled, giving me away.

"Don't be stubborn. You aren't any good to me as my assistant if you pass out from starvation." Jack's voice was insistent. "It's a little Italian place located just around the corner. The owner grew up in Rome. I'm telling you, he makes the best sauce in the entire state of California. Come on, you'll love it."

My stomach rumbled again, forcing me to concede. I thought Jack would want to drive that fancy sports car of his, but we walked instead, and I was pleasantly surprised when he stopped in front of Fabrizio's Pizzeria and opened the door for me.

"A pizza joint?" I laughed merrily.

"Of course. There's no place better."

We found a table tucked away near the back, and Jack ordered a large pizza with everything and a couple of beers.

"They brew their own beer here. It's really good," Jack boasted as the waiter set two frosted mugs on the table in front of us, and I laughed again.

"What's so funny?" Jack frowned with curiosity.

"I don't know," I flushed. "I guess I expected your favorite Italian restaurant to be some fancy place with cloth napkins and crystal glasses for the wine, not a place like this."

"Everyone always assumes I'm a big snob just because I made a little money with my security program. But I didn't grow up with a silver spoon in my mouth."

"A little money?" I arched my left brow skeptically.

"Okay, a lot of money," Jack conceded with chagrin, "but that doesn't change who I am on the inside. I might wear nicer clothes now and live in a bigger house, but I still like the same things I always did. Playing with computers, eating pizza, and..."

"Listening to cheesy classic rock." I finished his sentence for him.

"Listening to only the finest classic rock," Jack corrected me. We both laughed.

The waiter brought over our pizza, and it truly was delicious.

"You were right, this has to be the best sauce in California," I said as I wiped cheese off my chin. "Did you eat here a lot growing up?"

"Me? No. We could never afford to eat at a place like this. My father was often between jobs and he didn't like to let my mother work, so all our groceries usually came from food banks and assistance programs."

"I'm sorry." I suddenly felt bad for prying into something so personal, but none of the articles about him ever revealed that he grew up in poverty. Jack held himself with such refinement, it was easy to assume he was from a privileged background.

"No need to apologize. I'm not ashamed of where I came from. A kid can't help who his parents are when he's born, and I don't believe in shaming kids for being poor. It's why I created a charity program at the schools in my old neighborhood, elementary through high school. I want to make sure all those kids have pride in themselves and know they can accomplish anything if they're willing to work enough at it."

"I heard you gave scholarships to college students, but I didn't know you did charity work for younger kids too," I said with awe.

"I know from personal experience that it takes a lot of guts and effort to climb up from poverty and become a success, but it's not impossible. I want to instill in kids at every age to believe in themselves and to let them know there are adults out there who truly care about them. No kid can be expected to concentrate at school if they're hungry or cold or worried about being evicted onto the streets."

"Did that ever happen to you?" Before I could stop myself, I reached out and touched his hand. He didn't recoil.

"No, but we came close a few times," he said.

My heart went out to him. It wasn't pity that I felt but a deep sense of honor that he was sharing his personal story with me. It made me feel closer to him in ways that were deeply intimate, and I finally understood why he often put a hard shell around himself. I was honored now that he was letting me have a peek at the giving, caring man inside.

"My father was an alcoholic and an abusive asshole," Jack continued. "The landlord knew it, and I think he took pity on me and my mother, so he gave us more time to pay our back rent than he probably would have normally. I did end up living on the streets for a while though when I left home."

"What happened?" I asked, and he told me the horrifying tale about his father and the night he stood up to him when he was just seventeen years old. His own mother sided with his abuser and he'd been forced to leave home.

"So I walked out the door and never looked back. I haven't seen either of my parents since," Jack said with a haunted look in his deep blue eyes.

"I'm so sorry you had to go through all that," I said. My voice was thick with compassion. Moved and surprised by his story, I felt the sting of tears in my eyes, but I willed them to stay away. I didn't want him to see me cry.

"So, enough about me. Tell me about your childhood." Jack suddenly changed the subject with a jocular air, obviously trying to lighten the mood. "What was life like growing up in Iowa?"

"Oh, wow, my problems were nothing compared to yours." I ran my hands through my hair, pushing it back from my face.

"Good. Tell me about it," Jack said with sincere interest. "I really want to know."

"Well, my mom didn't work either, but not because Dad wouldn't let her. She liked being a housewife and a mother, and she was good at it. Dad sold insurance in an office downtown. Both my parents were very traditional, and they wanted me and my little sister, Jessica, to be the same way. It was always assumed that we would marry nice men who would provide for us while we raised the children." I paused to take a sip of my beer. I looked out the window, thinking of my family so many miles away. "Mom and Dad are so proud of Jessica. At the age of twenty-four, my little sister is already happily married with two perfect kids."

"I'm sure they're proud of you too." Jack leaned forward, his blue eyes twinkling.

"Not really. They consider me to be the rebellious daughter." It was something I had never confessed to anyone, not even Stuart. It hurt too much to say aloud that my parents were disappointed in me, but with Jack, I felt like I could tell him the painful truth. After all, his relationship with his parents had been so much worse, it helped me put my troubles in perspective.

"If you're as sassy with them as you are at the office, I can see why they'd feel that way," Jack teased. I threw my napkin at him, hitting him in the chest with it.

"My parents' idea of a sassy attitude was when I wanted to go to business school and have an independent career," I said. "It drove my parents crazy. They made me take etiquette classes so I could learn how to properly fold a dinner napkin and arrange flowers. When I got kicked out of class for arguing with the teacher, my parents finally relented and let me pursue a business degree at the community college. I had this crazy idea that I could run my own jewelry business someday."

"What kind of jewelry?"

"Stuff like this. I enjoy making jewelry during my time off. It's fun, and it helps me unwind." I stuck out my arm and let him see the bracelet I was wearing comprised of little hearts. He looked at the design carefully, raising his eyebrows in surprise.

"It's really nice. I see a lot of the women in the office wearing things that are similar," Jack commented casually, and I couldn't help but beam with pride.

"I made those. I hope you don't mind if I sell a few pieces every now and then. I promise, it doesn't interfere with work. Jewelry sales are strictly during breaks or after work." I held up my hand in a *Scout's honor* gesture.

"I don't mind, as long you don't leave me to become a famous jewelry designer. I need you too much," Jack said.

His words warmed my heart. It was good to know he needed me, even if it was just as his assistant and not more.

Although... the way he gazed at me so intensely made me wonder.

Laughing off his compliment, I said, "Don't worry, I gave up on that dream a long time ago. My parents would both die if I tried to be an entrepreneur. They have a hard enough time accepting the fact that I want to work in an office in LA and support myself. They never believed I could do it. They still don't, but I'm going to prove to them just how wrong they are."

"I'm sure you will," Jack said. "I bet they're prouder of you than you think they are."

"I doubt it. They keep pushing for me to marry this farmer named Mark Hansen so he can take care of me. But I can take care of myself. Which is why I escaped to LA and ended up getting this job working for you."

"I'm so glad you did," Jack said tenderly.

His eyes were two liquid pools as he gazed at my face. An intense, electric energy grew between us.

Was it possible? Did Jack truly feel something for me the way that I felt something for him? I wanted him so much, but the idea was too good to be true.

Just because he had shared with me the most intimate stories of his past, and I'd shared mine with him, didn't mean he was falling for me. He was my boss, maybe even my friend now, but he would never feel anything for me beyond the camaraderie of a boss with his employee. Anything else I thought I saw was purely my own fantasy.

We finished eating and walked back to the office, side by side, our hands nearly touching as we matched each other's stride. There was something incredibly comfortable about it. The atmosphere between us had changed now that we knew such intimate stories about each other's pasts.

As we approached the office, Jack stopped and looked at me, his gaze boring into my eyes as if we could see directly into each other's souls.

"Listen," he said awkwardly, "I wanted to thank you for letting me rattle on tonight about my shitty childhood and my abusive father. I didn't mean to lay so much heavy stuff on you."

"It's okay, really," I said, and his shoulders visibly relaxed.

"I think it was all the work we've been doing these past few days, focusing on family and how important it is. It got me thinking about my past and how I don't really have a family."

"Trust me, having a family isn't necessarily that great," I joked, trying to lighten the mood. Jack cracked a small smile, but his eyes were still troubled, like still water at night. "You may not have had a traditional family like mine, but you're not alone. Everyone at Lion is your family. Your employees care very deeply about you."

Those last words came out softly, like a whisper, and my heart began to pound. Could he read between the lines? Did he know how I felt about him?

"I care about them too," Jack said, his voice a husky whisper.

His face leaned in toward mine, and I raised my chin, our lips moving closer. We were about to kiss when suddenly the doors to the office building flew open. A string of employees exited, chatting happily among themselves as they walked toward their cars. It was the end of the work day, and they were all going home.

Jack and I stepped back and looked at one another. The magic spell of our almost kiss was broken, and neither of us knew what to do with our hands, shoving them nervously into pockets as we shuffled our feet with embarrassment.

"Looks like it's quitting time," Jack said, stating the obvious. "I didn't realize it was so late. Why don't you go ahead and go home too? I can finish preparing the sales pitch on my own."

"Are you sure? Because I don't mind the overtime," I said.

"Yeah, I'm sure," Jack said after a long and thoughtful pause.

He was right. It was better if we didn't tempt fate. He was my boss and I was his assistant. Just knowing we had almost kissed would have to be enough for me.

I gave him a timid wave goodbye and then I got in my car. I drove away with a smile on my face and a tear in my eye.

CHAPTER 9

JACK

"I've never been to this kind of a business meeting before. Do I look okay?" Violet approached me outside the bar with a nervous look on her lovely face.

She was wearing a little satin black dress that was simple yet elegant, adorned with silver jewelry that I now recognized as being her own creative work. A thin belt accented her skinny waist, and black pumps made her sexy legs look even longer and more sumptuous. Her mane of chestnut curls fell loosely to her shoulders, and her make-up had been enhanced to give her a smoky eye. The overall look was classy and alluring.

"You look more than okay. You look incredible," I breathed, and her face lit up at the compliment.

I'd been purposefully avoiding her all day, ever since we'd almost kissed last night. I didn't know how I could have let myself come so close to doing something so inappropriate, but at least nothing had happened between us. Now that I knew I couldn't be trusted to be alone with her, I had to be sure never to put myself in that tempting situation again.

So, I'd spent the whole day locked away in my office

under the guise of preparing for tonight's meeting with Howard Morris. Only now I couldn't avoid her any more. I'd already told him Violet and Grayson would both be at the meeting. It would look unprofessional if all three of us weren't there now, so I asked Grayson to drive her and meet me at the bar.

"How about me?" Grayson did a stylish turn. "Do I look okay?"

"You look like the same asshole you've always been," I said.

"You too," Grayson teased back.

Then I smacked my briefcase and said with a grin, "Let's get this show on the road."

The waitress seated us at our table, and we reviewed the game plan one last time. I was nervous as hell, but I thought I was doing a decent job of hiding it. I couldn't wait for Morris and his associates to arrive to put an end to this nervous waiting, but when they did, it only increased the pressure that I felt inside.

I waved the waitress over and ordered a round of drinks for the table to take the edge off, but I was surprised when she looked vaguely familiar.

"My sister, Ashley, sends her regards," the waitress said to me as she set the drinks on the table.

Shit. That's why I recognized her! She was the sister of that blonde Grayson set me up with that one night. I'd forgotten all about her since I blocked her number from my phone.

The waitress smiled. "She's here tonight if you want to get together for drinks later."

I glanced down at the end of the bar and saw her sitting there in a dress that was way too short and much too tight. She smiled and waved at me, and I just turned my back on her.

I whispered to the waitress so the others wouldn't hear, "Tell Ashley I'm sorry, but we can't date each other."

"It's okay, she knows you're in a meeting. She'll just wait till it's over."

"Great," I muttered to myself. Now, on top of the pressure of the biggest sales meeting of my life, I had the added stress of a stalker waiting for me. I turned my attention to Howard Morris and said, "Shall we begin?"

He said easily, "I don't usually agree to meet with just anybody who calls me up out of the blue, but what you had to say intrigued me. I must admit, I'm curious to hear more about what Lion, Inc., has to offer."

All eyes at the table turned to me as I presented our pitch for how Lion could provide superior cybersecurity to Vista Hotels for everything from guest information and credit card payments to payroll and employee privacy. The references to his family seemed to especially hit home with Morris, and I made a mental note to thank Violet for suggesting it.

"What you've shown here tonight is impressive," Howard Morris said when I was finished, and I felt my heart rate quicken. "But I'm just not sure if I'm ready to sign on. I'll have to discuss this with my associates and get back to you."

My heart fell as quickly as it had risen. *I'll get back to you* usually meant *no*. As Morris started to get up from the table, Violet put a delicate hand on his arm and stopped him. Speaking softly, she asked, "Do you mind telling me what you're unsure about?"

Violet had a way of getting hardened businessmen to open up to her. At least I knew she had that effect on me. As Morris talked about his concerns, she listened intently and was able to address each one of them with intelligence and confidence. By the end, Morris was smiling as he shook her hand and said, "You know, young lady, you've convinced me to go with Lion."

He looked at his associates, and they all nodded in agreement.

"Thank you. You won't regret it." Violet's smile lit up the room. She went over the service contract with him and Morris signed it right there at the table, handing Violet a sizable check for the first month's service.

As he left, Morris looked at me and said, "If all your employees are as bright as her, I know I'll get excellent service."

"Well, Violet is one of a kind, but I promise you, I'll have the very best engineers protecting your hotels twenty-four hours a day."

We shook hands and he left with a smile on his face.

"We did it!" Grayson shouted out with relief and joy.

"Thanks to Violet," I said, and she blushed at the compliment. I waved over the waitress and said, "This calls for a toast to celebrate!"

I was about to order a bottle of scotch from the waitress when I saw her chatting with her sister. Damn. The last thing I wanted was for Ashley to come over and sit with us now that the meeting was over. If that happened, I might not ever get rid of her.

"Let's go to my place. I've got a bottle of thirty-year aged scotch I've been saving for just this kind of occasion," I announced as the idea struck me. Then I turned to Grayson and said, "Do you mind settling the bill at the register for me?"

Grayson glanced over and caught sight of Ashley. I could tell he instantly understood. "No problem," he said. "You two go ahead to your place. I'll take care of the bill and be right behind you."

Ah, shit. I hadn't realized my plan would mean Violet and I would be alone together, and I never told Grayson about the kiss we'd almost shared together. At the time, I didn't want Grayson to give me crap about it, but now there was no way for me to bail out on my own invite without raising suspicion.

"Sounds good," I said, praying Grayson really would arrive to my place quickly.

"YOUR HOUSE IS AMAZING," Violet gasped in awe as I pulled the Porsche into the garage and guided her inside. In the kitchen, I grabbed the bottle of scotch from the liquor cabinet and loaded a bucket with some ice while Violet rummaged through my cupboards looking for the glasses.

We carried everything into the sitting room where I took my time lighting a fire in the fireplace, stalling for time until Grayson arrived. Silence stretched out between us. When Violet cleared her throat for the third time, I could tell she felt as awkward as I did.

"Maybe I should just have a cab take me home," she finally said.

I realized I was being unreasonable. So what if I'd nearly kissed her yesterday? We'd been discussing a lot of intimate stuff, and I was feeling particularly vulnerable. Plus, I was exhausted from working my ass off all week on the sales pitch. It was no wonder I faltered in a moment of weakness, but that didn't mean it would ever happen again. I was a professional CEO, and Violet and I had been alone together countless times before without incident.

We deserved this celebration. I'd promised her a toast with my premium scotch, and I wasn't going to back out just because I found her sexually attractive.

"Grayson's always late. Forget that son of a bitch and let's celebrate without him!" I said to Violet with a chuckle. I opened the scotch and filled two glasses. Raising mine up in the air, I gazed at Violet and said, "To a job well done!"

"To us!" Violet clinked her glass against mine. Her eyes grew wide as she swallowed the liquid. "Wow, this really is good."

"I told you, this is the way to celebrate." I laughed and poured us each another.

"It's too bad Grayson is missing out," Violet said.

"Yeah, where is that asshole?" I grabbed my phone to call him and saw that he'd already sent me a text. I must have missed hearing the notification.

Met a total babe while paying the bill. I'm staying at the bar and celebrating with her instead. Sorry, bro.

"It looks like it's just us after all," I said, and my throat grew tight as I read the text to Violet.

"I'm sorry you wasted your good scotch on just me. I know you were saving it for something special," Violet said, half serious and half apologetic. She looked so beautiful sitting there in the glow of the firelight, I had to tell her how I felt, even though I knew I shouldn't.

"You *are* something special, and tonight is not a waste," I insisted. I reached out to delicately touch her chin so I could raise her face to meet my gaze. "You work harder than anybody I know at Lion, and not just on the Vista Hotel pitch, but every day. I know you're the first to arrive every morning and the last to leave. You may not think anybody notices how hard you work and how smart you are, but I do."

"Really?" Violet's face lit up.

I swallowed as my eyes wandered to her chest. I could see her breasts heaving under the fabric of her clothing. She drew closer to me and put her hand on my chest.

Fuck.

I could feel the heat emanating between us as my cock strained in my pants. If she was going to put her delicate little hand on my chest like that, I wouldn't be able to hold back.

The temptation to kiss her was unbearable, and I moved closer. I couldn't fight it any longer.

Suddenly, Violet closed the distance between us, reaching for me. I pressed my mouth to her soft lips. Her mouth opened, letting me in. I ran my hands through her lush hair, holding her to me, as I kissed her deeply.

She tasted even better than I'd dreamed. Her breasts felt so soft as they crushed against my chest.

She whimpered softly, and I pulled her closer. I moved my hands down to her round ass and squeezed it as I pressed my hard cock against her.

"I need you, Violet," I said as I breathed her in.

"Take me to bed," she moaned breathlessly.

My mind was screaming at me to step away, but my body didn't care. Tonight, my most taboo fantasy was coming true.

CHAPTER 10

VIOLET

"*I* need you *now*, Violet. Let's do it right here," he murmured as he kissed my neck.

I nodded breathlessly.

He unzipped my dress, which fell to my feet. I kicked it across the floor. Jack's hands slid up my torso and he cupped my breasts over my bra. My nipples tingled and grew taut beneath his touch. I sighed with pleasure as he bent to kiss the swell of my breast. His hands moved to the small of my back, and he pulled me to him abruptly. I lost my balance for a moment, suddenly dizzy with desire for him, but he caught me and held me in his strong hands.

"Got you," he whispered with a smile.

He traced a line down my neck then buried his face in my cleavage and kissed me. My entire body quivered with pleasure. An unquenchable desire erupted inside me, and I wanted more.

I struggled to unclasp my bra. He helped me, peeling the lacy fabric away from my body and tossing it aside, so my bare breasts were now exposed to him.

"You are so beautiful," he whispered. He filled his hands

and then his mouth with my bare breasts, kissing and suckling them until I was panting and moaning with pleasure. My panties became soaked with the fluids of my desire. Sliding his hand down my hips, he slowly peeled them off.

"I want you," I gasped, as I started peeling off his clothes, eager to see his bare body. He unbuttoned and removed his shirt as I watched, biting my lip.

His torso was like a masterpiece, rippling with muscles. I ran my hands over his pectorals and chiseled abs, and he drew in his breath with pleasure.

Finally, I pulled down his pants and boxers, revealing the treasure hidden beneath. His cock was large and fully erect. I grasped the shaft, stroking him with my hands before lowering myself to my knees.

I looked up at him as I licked the tip of his cock.

"Oh, fuck," he growled.

I took him fully into my mouth, keeping my eyes locked on his. I took his length into my mouth and throat. Jack groaned with ecstasy as he ran his hands through my hair, wanting more. He pushed his length gently inside my mouth, closing his eyes from pleasure. It gave me a surge of excitement to know that I was the one making him feel so good.

"Now it's my turn." Jack grinned when I released him from my hot, wet mouth.

He had me lie down on the soft, luxurious carpet in front of his fireplace and spread my thighs wide. His tongue lapped at me gently, teasing my outer lips and clitoris. Then he licked me with more pressure, sending a shudder of delight through my body.

"That feels so good, Jack," I murmured. He didn't stop as he licked me hungrily while rubbing my clit with his thumb. Then he slid two fingers inside me, pushing them all the way inside. The intensity built inside my core as he licked me. It was amazing, but I wanted more. I wanted him inside me.

"Fuck me now!" I screamed aloud as he brought me to near orgasm with his fingers and tongue.

He pulled back to look at me for a moment and then he slid a condom over his length. He entered me slowly, plunging his rock-hard member into my folds with measured force, deeper and deeper, as he massaged my clitoris with his thumb. The pleasure was unbelievable, and I grasped and clawed at his chest, wanting all of him at once, but he took his time, drawing out my pleasure with incredible patience. I shuddered as a wave of dizzying heat washed over me. I had no idea my body was capable of experiencing such intense pleasure.

"I'm coming!" I cried aloud, and he closed his mouth over mine, taking me with a passionate kiss as his member plunged the rest of the way inside me. My hips thrust wildly, desperate to be fucked by him, and he slowly began to thrust inside me, kissing me all the while. I surrendered into the explosive feeling inside me, closing my eyes and savoring the moment.

My arms and legs wrapped around him, twisting like a vine around a tree trunk, as I luxuriated in the feel of having such a magnificent man inside me. My body calmed its frenzy, and I allowed myself to find his pace and match his rhythm. Our bodies moved together as one, flexing and plunging in perfect symmetry. The pleasure was unlike anything I'd experienced before as it rose up to newer and greater heights, and I orgasmed yet again.

"Keep coming for me," Jack whispered as I experienced my second orgasm – or was it still the same one growing more powerful within me? I didn't know, and I no longer cared. The world around me melted away, and all I could experience was pleasure.

I gyrated wildly beneath him. My eyes moved up his toned, tight torso to his intense eyes. He closed them for a moment as the sensations overpowered him, and I could tell he was getting closer.

He thrust inside me more forcefully, his hand moving over one of my breasts and then the other. He lifted my legs over his shoulders so he could go deeper. I moaned in pleasure and bit my lip.

"You like it when I'm deep inside you?" he asked breathlessly.

I nodded my head. "Yes. I love it."

He slid inside me again, and it hit that magical place deep inside that made me cry out in pleasure. I felt his cock throb inside me.

"Oh, God," I moaned. He bent down to kiss me just as another orgasm began to wash over me. I gave in to the waves that rocked through my core, and I gasped. I opened my eyes to see his locked on mine. He groaned and thrust deeply inside.

"Come for me, Jack," I said.

He pushed himself inside me to the hilt and emptied his release with a primal cry. His cock throbbed deep inside my walls as he came.

Finally, he gently lay on me, kissing me tenderly.

"You're incredible, Violet," he said as he pulled away a bit to look at me.

I smiled. "You are, too, Jack. That was amazing." I shifted a little, and his cock was getting hard again inside me. "And I can tell you're ready for more."

He grinned and thrust himself deeper inside. "I can't get enough of you."

We were at it all night long. First in front of the fireplace, then on the sofa, and eventually we moved to his luxurious bedroom.

My hands clutched the bedpost as he fucked me powerfully from behind, and then we had sex again more gently, lying side-by-side on the giant mattress, wrapped in his lavish satin sheets.

It was a fantasy come true, and I kept wondering if I was dreaming, but I knew I wasn't.

Neither of us wanted the night to end. Because by morning, the fantasy would end as well. And we'd both have to face that what we were doing was wrong.

CHAPTER 11

JACK

"*V*iolet?" I stretched out my arms as I yawned myself awake and discovered the other half of the bed was empty.

Shit! What had I done last night? I'd fucked up, that was for sure!

I couldn't believe I'd broken the first rule of being a boss. Never sleep with an employee.

Only this was far worse. I hadn't just slept with Violet Williams once in a drunken moment of passion. I had sex with her multiple times, in multiple positions, all night long, leaving a trail of condoms in our wake. Shit! What the hell had I been thinking?

I knew exactly what I'd been thinking. Violet was beautiful, interesting, and the most incredibly sexy woman I'd ever known. Everything about her turned me on, from her wit to her skin-tight skirts. It was a miracle I hadn't made a move on her sooner, but I was her boss, and that meant denying my own personal desires for the greater good of my company. I couldn't selfishly fuck any woman I found sexually attractive. That was how sex scandals and harassment lawsuits happened.

Oh, shit! What if Violet filed a complaint or pressed charges? Or worst of all, what if she quit? I couldn't stand the thought of losing her. She wasn't just the best assistant I'd ever worked with, she was the best part of my job. I loved seeing her smiling face every day and the way she lit up the office with her spirit and her attitude. She was a breath of fresh air, and I knew I would suffocate without her.

I moved to the kitchen, ready to face the music. But she wasn't there. I turned down the hall toward the living room, expecting to find her lounging on the couch with a book. My heart raced as I approached.

This was all my fault. Sure, she had kissed me first, but I had brought her to my home and plied her with liquor and flirty banter. I was a man who could take responsibility for his own actions. I was the one who had fucked up. Now I had to make things right.

I searched the house frantically, but it was clear she had left.

This was not a good sign.

I tried calling her cell, but it went right to voicemail. Dressing quickly, I got in my car and raced to the office, hoping she was there and it wasn't too late to discuss things.

"Good morning, Mr. McCann," the receptionist greeted me.

"Hi, Kate. How many times must I tell you to call me Jack? I want everyone here to feel like family."

"Yes, Mr. McCann," Kate replied.

"Ugh, just forget it." I sighed. "I'm going to be in my office. Please notify me the moment Violet Williams arrives to work."

"She's already here." Kate nodded her head towards the programmers' cubicles.

Violet was talking with Maddie, her head bent forward, whispering low in her ear. Maddie covered her mouth with her hands to stifle a gasp and immediately looked over at me.

Shit. I was officially fucked.

"Good morning, ladies." I approached them quickly, interrupting their conversation. How much had Violet told Maddie? How did she feel about what had happened last night? My heart was pounding so hard in my fucking chest, I could hardly hear myself think over the noise.

"Good morning," Violet said easily. "Did you need something?"

She was so relaxed and casual, it was as if nothing had happened between us.

"Yes, I need to talk to you in my office," I said, exuding a fake confidence I absolutely did not feel. I was terrified it was obvious to the whole room that I was acting and behaving strangely, but nobody gave any indication they knew anything about me and Violet having had sex.

Fuck. I needed to quit being so paranoid or people would notice and start asking questions.

"Hey, buddy, there you are," Grayson called out to me, his voice booming. "Late night celebrating?"

"What? Me? No, of course not," I stammered like a fucking idiot.

He sidled up to me and lowered his voice.

"Sorry I stood you up, but I ended up going home with that redhead last night," Grayson bragged with a wink. All I could do was grin and nod like I wasn't hiding something. Grayson put his hand on my shoulder and said, "Do you want to announce to the company that we landed the Vista Hotel account, or should I?"

"I don't care," I snapped. Grayson looked at me with a surprised frown. Softening my tone, I said, "It was more of a group effort. Why don't you make the announcement? I have something I need to take care of in my office."

As the room erupted with cheers over Grayson's announcement, I turned to Violet and led her into my office.

"We need to talk about last night," I said to her once the door was locked and the shades were drawn.

"We sure do," Violet said.

I swallowed. I was in deep shit.

CHAPTER 12

VIOLET

Three hours earlier

𝒥 woke up in Jack's arms, still tingling from the incredible night of orgasms he'd given me.

It had been the best night of my life. I never knew my body was capable of such rapture, and to experience it again and again was even more amazing.

But as the morning light entered the room, a lump grew in my throat. I'd made a horrible mistake. I'd thrown myself at my boss and asked him to take me to bed.

I could have stayed in his arms forever, but I had to leave.

As I quietly gathered my clothes and got dressed, my hands began to shake.

There was no way I'd be able to keep my job after this.

I knew Jack wouldn't fire me. He was much too noble for that. But how could we keep working together after this? Surely, he would have me transferred somewhere, and I didn't want that. I loved working for him. Being an EA at an important company like Lion made me feel valued, like what I did meant something to people's daily lives.

I slipped outside and waited for an Uber to arrive. Fifteen minutes later, I got dropped off at my car in the parking garage at work.

With a defeated sigh, I sat behind the driver's seat and started my vehicle. I'd ruined everything.

The humiliation was still etched all over my face as I did the walk of shame into my apartment building, carrying my heels in one hand and my purse in the other. My hair was a tangled mess, and my smeared mascara made me look like a dead raccoon.

"There you are!" Stuart ran forward to hug me, then stopped short with his hands on his hips. "Oh, sweetie, please tell me you did what I think you did last night."

"I don't have time to talk about it," I moaned. "I have to get ready for work or I'll be late. That is, if I still have a job."

"Ah! That means you *did* do it!" Stuart cried out excitedly. "You slept with Mr. Sexiest Bachelor CEO! Tell me everything! I want to know every last detail."

"Leave me alone, Stuart!" I begged, but my nosy roommate kept grilling me with questions, even as I took a shower and tried to get dressed.

"Does he look as good naked as he looks in a suit? Is he hairy? Does he have any tattoos?"

I ignored all his questions. I was so mad at myself for my own foolishness. How on earth could I have slept with the boss from hell? What was wrong with me? Well, now I'd have to face what I'd done. I might as well begin with my roommate.

"Enough!" I finally said, turning to Stuart with a hairbrush and pleading eyes. "I'll tell you everything you want to know if you'll just help me with my hair. It'll take me all day to get these tangles out alone."

Stuart styled and curled while I talked. It felt good to get everything off my chest. I hated secrets, and most of all I hated people who wouldn't face up to their mistakes. I knew I needed to take responsibility for this one.

"So, what are you going to do now?" Stuart asked when I was all dressed and ready to leave for work.

"I'm going to march right into Jack's office and tell him that last night was a big mistake. Then, I'm going to convince him not to get rid of me," I said bravely.

"Don't worry sweetie, he can't do that. It would be sexual harassment."

"I know, but he could transfer me to be someone else's assistant, and I don't want that. I've worked hard to be an assistant to the CEO, and anything else would be like being demoted. I love my job. I don't want to lose it."

"Then get out there and fight for it."

"Thanks, Stuart," I said as he hugged me for support, being careful not to wrinkle my outfit. Then, I charged out the door.

When I got to work, Jack wasn't there yet, and I was relieved to have a chance to talk to Maddie.

"Here, I made these for you." I handed her a set of jewelry I'd been working on ever since the Howard Morris pitch began. It was a necklace, bracelet, and matching earrings, all with the adorable little hearts that made me so happy.

"This is beautiful!" Maddie gasped in surprise and immediately started putting everything on. "I love them! I don't have any cash in my purse to pay you for them, but I'll get some during my lunch break today."

"No, these are my gift to you," I insisted.

"Did you already forget what I told you about valuing your work?" Maddie chastised.

"I didn't, but I also know the value of friendship, and the time we've spent together is more valuable than money. So I wanted you to have these as my way of showing you how I feel about you."

I also wanted to give them to her now in case I never got to see her again. But I couldn't tell her that.

Maddie had to blink back tears of emotion as she hugged me tight. "Thank you. I love these hearts as much as I love you. If you won't let me pay for the necklace and bracelet, at least let me give you something for the earrings."

"Oh, you already did. When the other programmers saw the pi pendant I made you, several of them asked if I could make one for them. I got half a dozen sales, just like you predicted."

"I keep telling you, your jewelry could turn into a stellar business if you ever wanted to sell it on a larger scale. I could show you how to create your own web store, and you could work right from home."

"I might need to," I said cryptically.

"What's going on? Are you quitting?" Maddie gasped and covered her face.

Just then, I looked over and saw that Jack had entered the room.

Just seeing him again made my body quiver with excitement. I straightened my spine and tried to act like nothing had happened between us. When he told me he needed to speak to me, my heart dropped like a stone.

I followed him into his office, hiding my shaking hands behind my back to maintain a cool facade. When he locked the door and closed the shades, I knew I was in big trouble. Nobody could seduce the CEO of their company and expect to get away with it unscathed.

Jack was going to transfer me away.

The thought filled me with dread. I loved this job. More than that, I couldn't bear the idea of not seeing Jack every day. Even if we never slept together again, I wanted to be near him, to be his friend. Jack was far more than just a grouchy boss, he was a brilliant man with a huge heart.

My only hope to keep from being transferred was to be completely up front with him. I needed to own up to my mistake, to apologize for getting drunk and throwing myself at him, and to promise to never behave so outrageously again. Maybe then, there was a chance he would forgive me and let me stay.

As we faced off, the tension in the air was so thick, it was hard to breathe.

I just prayed I could say what I needed to say before I passed out from a lack of oxygen.

"We need to talk about last night," Jack said ominously.

"We sure do," I said with a gulp.

"It was a mistake," we both blurted out at once.

"Wait. What did you say?" Jack's handsome face had gone pale with shock.

"I made a terrible mistake last night, getting drunk and then throwing myself at you," I said, twisting my hands. "I never should have acted so disgracefully. I'm sorry."

"You have nothing to be sorry about," Jack said, his eyes dark with emotion. "The fault was entirely mine. It was a mistake for me to drive you out to my house, give you scotch, and then sleep with you. I'm the one who's sorry."

"I guess maybe we're both to blame," I said cautiously.

"No, I'm the CEO and you're the employee. The buck stops with me. I accept full responsibility," Jack said firmly.

"I'm not going to let you run over top of me just because you're the CEO," I shot back. "If you were willing to give me credit for all the hard work I did on the Vista Hotel pitch, then you also need to share the blame for what happened last night."

"Fine. We're both to blame," Jack acquiesced unhappily.

"Thank you," I said curtly.

Suddenly, the absurdity of our argument occurred to me, and I broke into a smile. Then a laugh.

"You're welcome." Jack grinned, and then we were laughing together. It was a release from the tension we'd both been feeling and something we both desperately needed.

As the laughter died down, Jack looked at me with a grave expression and said softly, "Seriously though, I truly am sorry for my inappropriate behavior. You're the best EA I've ever worked with, and I don't want to lose you. Is there anything I can do to get you to stay?"

My heart was soaring as I drew in a heavy breath of relief. "You still want me to stay? I was terrified you'd want to transfer me away so you wouldn't have to look at me anymore."

Jack's lips curved into a sexy smile as he said playfully, "Trust me, I would never not want to look at you." Then he shook his head as if reprimanding himself, and said sternly, "That's the kind of thing that got us into this mess. I promise that from now on I'll keep things strictly professional between us."

"Me too," I vowed sincerely. "No more jokes or teasing."

"No more intimate talks, no more drinks alone together," Jack said.

"No more dining alone or dancing to rock music," I added to the list, even as we both smiled wistfully at the memory.

"From this moment on, we are strictly work associates. Employer and employee. We will treat each other with respect and professionalism, and nothing more will happen between us."

"Agreed."

I shook his hand with formal detachment, meeting his eyes only for a second before I looked away. With a quick nod, I turned and left.

As I walked back to my desk, I should have felt relieved. Our agreement had been the best outcome I could have wished for. Jack shared in the responsibility of our mistake. He didn't want to transfer me. My position as his EA was safe. I'd gotten everything I'd wanted.

Well, not everything. Even as I walked from Jack's office, having just seen him, I was already missing him. He looked so handsome with his deep blue eyes imploring me to stay. I already longed for the feel of his mouth on my body, the incredible sensation of his manhood entering my body, and the rapturous ecstasy of climaxing with him.

When I reached my desk, I glanced over my shoulder and caught sight of him. He was standing at the window in his office, pulling the shades open. His eyes landed on me, and he stood there just a little too long, watching me.

The look in his eyes told me everything I needed to know. A smile creased my lips, and he grinned back at me.

Yes, our vow to keep things professional was already doomed.

CHAPTER 13

JACK

"You wanted to see me?" Violet's voice was a seductive purr that drove me wild with desire.

"Yes, I need copies of these for the meeting this afternoon," I said, handing her a stack of papers. Our hands touched, and I felt a jolt of electricity zip through me like crackling passion igniting into flame.

Her skin was soft, her perfume intoxicating. I should have made a rule that she couldn't wear it. But if I did that, I'd have to ban her entire wardrobe. Everything she wore, from her body-skimming skirts to her silky blouses, made me want to take her into my arms and fuck her all night long, just like we did that night in my house.

Every day since then, I'd come to work determined to resist the lure of her raw sexuality. I walked into work, focused on treating her with professional distance. But every time I saw her, I failed.

Her smile, her beautiful eyes when they looked at me, everything about her exuded sensuality, and I was helpless to resist. I'd never wanted anybody more. I had to have her again, and it was obvious she wanted me too.

She kept doing little things to entice me. A touch of her hand, a caress on my shoulder. Several times, she made a point of getting a little too close so I could feel her breasts brush against me. Seeing her now, I wanted to pull her into my embrace and fuck her on my desk until I made her come.

I needed to go for a walk to clear my head.

I exited my office and paced around the building under the pretense of checking up on the programmers. Violet passed by on her way to the copy room, and I purposefully averted my gaze. Maddie eyed me suspiciously, along with a few others, and I knew I had to get even further away from Violet before anyone guessed how much I secretly desired her.

I strode purposefully to the elevator, anxious to get outside for some fresh air, but moments before the door closed, a hand shot out and held the door open. It was Violet. Fuck.

She entered the elevator and pressed the button for the ground floor. Shit! In the confined space, there was no escaping. My desire for her overwhelmed me. Violet looked at me and licked her lips flirtatiously. It was all the permission I needed. I lunged at her, pressing her against the wall of the elevator, and kissed her passionately.

I wondered if I'd made a huge mistake and pulled back to see if I'd crossed a line and she was mad at me. In response, she flung her arms around me, drawing me to her, and returned the kiss with a fire that told me she wanted me just as much as I wanted her.

We clung to each other, devouring each other in a consuming kiss that made it impossible to breathe, and yet we couldn't stop. We both knew we only had until the elevator doors opened again, and we needed to make the most of what little time we had.

My heart dropped along with the elevator as it hit the

ground floor and the doors opened. We each walked off in separate directions, acting as if nothing had happened between us.

Violet was playing with fire. She'd fanned the flames inside me, and nothing would extinguish them except being inside her again.

I spent the rest of the day in my office with the doors locked and the shades drawn, trying to avoid her, but I couldn't keep that up forever. I had a business to run.

"Are you feeling all right today?" Grayson clasped me on the shoulder as we exited the conference room together after the meeting that afternoon.

"Yeah, of course I am," I lied. "Why, do I look like shit or something?"

"No, you've just been off your game for the past week," Grayson observed. "You've always been the meticulous one, but lately you're absentminded as fuck. You're late to meetings and making simple mistakes. It's not like you. I want to make sure everything is okay."

I knew better than to try to bullshit him. Grayson knew me better than anyone and would see right through any lie. The best thing I could do was to confess – just not the whole truth.

"I've been preoccupied with a woman, to be honest. She's so hot, I can't stop thinking about her. The problem is she's not available."

"Boyfriend?" Grayson asked.

I shook my head. "No, she's single. It's just complicated."

"How complicated can it be?" Grayson shrugged with a grin. "Give her some of that famous Jack McCann charm apparently no girl can resist. Take her to your place and give her the best night of sex she's ever had."

"I kinda already did," I said with chagrin. "It was unbelievable. She had me going all night long, and I still want more."

"A second date with the same woman?" Grayson shook his head and gave a low whistle of surprise. "That's big. You really do like her."

"I've been trying to forget about her, but it's not working. The harder I try to get her out of my head, the more I want to be with her again."

"Well, then stop fighting it," Grayson said wisely. "There's nothing stopping you from going out with this woman as many times as you want. You were the one that made the rule of no second dates, and you can break it."

"She's not available, like I said. She can't go out with me, even if I asked her to."

"I think that's up to her," Grayson said. "If you want her that much, go ahead and ask her. Let the decision be hers. If she wants you as much as you want her, then don't worry about what anybody else thinks. Go for it. You deserve to be happy for once."

I thanked Grayson and retreated to my office to think. I wanted to take his advice and run with it. But I also knew there was no fucking way he would have said any of those things if he'd known I was talking about an employee. Violet wasn't just any woman, she was my assistant, and that made her off limits, no matter how much I wanted things to be different.

I stayed locked in my office for the rest of the evening, waiting for Violet to go home for the night so I wouldn't risk seeing her and kissing her again. Finally, it was late enough I figured I was safe. I locked up the office and rode the elevator down to the parking garage, but as I walked towards my Porsche, I saw her standing there by her little blue Hyundai looking miserable.

"What are you doing here so late?" I asked with concern.

I figured her car wouldn't start or she'd lost her keys. Far be it for me to leave a damsel in distress, even one I was supposed to be avoiding.

"I was waiting for you," Violet's words surprised me. "I thought we should talk about that kiss in the elevator."

"Yeah. Sorry about that." I rubbed my hand on the back of my neck, trying to mask my shame. "The next time you need to use the elevator, I'll just take the stairs."

"No, don't do that. I wanted to tell you I liked it," Violet confessed, her eyes large. "It's been terrible not being with you all week. Torture, even." She took a step toward me.

"I felt the same way," I breathed. I took a step closer to her.

We were standing right against each other now, face to face, so close our faces were nearly touching.

"I've really missed you these past few days." Violet's voice was a soft whisper. "You spent so much time locked in your office, I thought maybe you were mad at me."

"What? No. It was the opposite," I cried out, and her shoulders dropped with a sigh of relief. Caressing her cheek, I said gently, "I had to force myself to keep away from you, because I knew if I let myself get too near, I'd kiss you. Just like what happened in the elevator."

"I already told you, I liked that." Violet circled her arms around my neck and turned her face toward mine, enticing me to kiss her.

My eyes glanced around the garage to see if anyone was watching us. We were completely alone. I gave in to my impulses and closed my mouth over hers, taking her in a passionate embrace. Her lips parted, welcoming my tongue as she kissed me back.

"I want you," I whispered in her ear as I kissed her neck. My hand slid down her waist to squeeze her sumptuous ass.

"I want you too," she panted with desire.

With no one around to stop us, I opened the passenger side door of my car. She got in, leaving her car behind, along with her inhibitions.

I sped all the way to my house, and we had half our clothes off before we even stepped inside the door.

"Are you sure you want to do this?" I asked before peeling off her bra.

"I'm sure," she insisted as she pulled down my pants.

Leaving our clothes behind in a pile on the floor, I picked her up in my arms as she squealed with laughter.

I carried her up the stairs to my bedroom, relieved that my wait to have her again was finally over.

Placing her gently on the bed, I took in the sight of her naked body before me.

"Come here, Jack," she purred with a grin.

CHAPTER 14

VIOLET

"You're all smiles today," Maddie noted as she peered at me over the rim of her spectacles. Her hair had changed overnight from blue to bright fuchsia pink and so had her glasses to match.

"Am I?" I feigned innocence while hiding my face behind a shuffle of papers, trying to act aloof.

She'd caught me thinking about the incredible marathon of sex Jack and I had shared again last night. The man had a magical gift. He could bring pleasures out of me beyond anything I'd ever dreamed. The more sex we had, the more I craved. Our appetites for each other were insatiable, and even now I was wondering when we could do it again.

Of course, last night we'd agreed it had to be the last time, but I knew we wouldn't last long.

"You haven't been able to quit grinning since the moment you got here, and I know why." Maddie pushed her fuchsia glasses back up her nose. She pointed her finger at me and said accusingly, "You got laid last night."

"What? No. Of course not! Where did you get a crazy idea like that?" I laughed it off, rather unconvincingly.

I'd always been a bad liar. It must have been all those Sunday school classes when I was kid. I didn't know why I even *attempted* to be deceitful. But Jack and I had promised each other we'd keep our affair a secret, so I had to try.

"You've had sex all right. The really good kind," Maddie said with a confident tilt of her chin. "The question is, who was the lucky guy?"

"That's none of your business," I snapped, accidentally revealing that she was right about me having sex. Ugh! Why couldn't I learn how to tell a white lie?

"You never go anywhere but work, and your roommate is gay. So, the odds are it's someone you met here in the office," Maddie said thoughtfully. She loved a good puzzle and never let one go until she solved it. It was only a matter of time before she realized I was sleeping with the boss, and I felt myself starting to panic.

"Maybe I'm just in a good mood because the pitch went so well with Howard Morris and Vista Hotels," I blabbered incoherently.

"I know who you slept with!" Maddie lit up, and I felt my heart sink to the pit of stomach like a stone. My worst nightmare came true when Maddie drew in her breath and cried out, "Jack!"

My blood pressure exploded in my chest, and I wondered if I was having a legitimate heart attack. Maddie had figured out my secret affair even faster than I thought she would.

Maddie used her eyes and a jerk of her head to indicate someone behind me, and I turned to see Jack standing right there.

Ah, thank goodness!

She didn't know I was sleeping with Jack; she simply called out his name because he had emerged from his office. I exhaled with relief.

As I tried to regain my composure, Jack looked at me and

barked, "Violet, I can't find the file for the Vista Hotel account that I had on my desk earlier this morning. I need that file, right now!"

I stiffened at his brusqueness.

"I have a copy of everything in my computer. I'll forward whatever you need right to you," I offered.

"No, the paper file had the copies with all my notes on them. A copy won't do me any good. I need those fucking notes!"

"The file was on your desk," I started to say, and he cut me off.

"It's not there now," he said, running a hand through his hair. "Never mind. I'll find it myself," he said as he stormed away.

I was immediately ruffled by his rude tone, but I took a breath and let the irritation dissipate. This account was so much bigger than any he'd had before. He was obviously acting out because he was under a mountain of stress, and my heart went out to him. I was about to say something sympathetic about him to Maddie when I realized this was the perfect opportunity to throw her off our trail.

"Jack is such a bosshole," I groaned with exasperation. "How am I supposed to know where he set some file? Talk about someone needing to get laid! Only I can't imagine any woman being able to put up with him long enough to do it."

"You don't think he's handsome?" Maddie looked at me with surprise.

I rolled my eyes and snorted with derision. "He'd be a lot better looking if he wasn't always so moody and crabby. I bet those papers he's looking for are right on his desk. I'd better help him find them before he has an epic meltdown."

"You're brave to make such a sacrifice for the rest of us," Maddie teased. "By the way, I ran your credit report like you asked me to. Your ex-boyfriend wasn't able to open any new accounts in your name."

"Good. I closed the accounts he's been using so he can't rack up any more debt in my name, and I made payment plans with all the creditors."

"Just give me the word and I'll make it so he'll never get a loan or credit card again for the rest of his life," Maddie said.

"Thanks, but I have a feeling he's already doing that all on his own."

"Suit yourself, but I'm impressed with how maturely you're handling this mess."

"Well, I figure even if I'm mired in debt, I'd still rather be living a great life in LA than in Iowa trapped in an unhappy marriage," I said with a wink.

From the corner of my eye, I caught sight of Jack striding into his office with the missing file in his hand. He still looked so stressed and miserable. I wanted to comfort him. I said to Maddie with a sigh, "Well, I'd better see if I can help the boss before he fires us all. I'll talk to you later."

I made sure Maddie had turned her attention back to her computer. Once she was deep in the coding zone, nothing could tear her away. Then, I casually slipped into Jack's office, closed the shades, and locked the door.

"What is it?" Jack snapped before he lifted his head. His face softened when he realized it was me.

"I see you found the missing contract," I said.

"I did. Sorry I snapped at you out there, Violet. I just have a lot on my mind making sure everything goes perfectly with this account, and I can't shake this feeling I'm missing something."

"Maybe you need to take a break from it. Come back to it with a fresh mind," I suggested with a salacious purr.

"Not now," Jack muttered. He didn't even look at me as I tried to seduce him by running my hands across my body.

Trying to gain his attention, I crossed the room and sat sexily on the edge of his desk. He just kept staring at the contract. "We need to set up the cybersecurity for each hotel individually so we don't miss anything. We're going to need to hire more people for sure. I want to get ahead of this thing so we're not caught with our pants down."

"Ooh, now that's good idea," I said. Jack looked shocked as I slid off his desk, pushed his chair back, and knelt down between his legs.

"What are you doing?" he gaped as I unbuckled his belt and starting unzipping his pants.

"I'm catching you with your pants down," I murmured.

"What? It's the middle of the workday," Jack started to object, but I silenced him when I brought my mouth to his cock and kissed him there, letting my tongue linger for an extra-long time.

"Don't worry," I said soothingly, "I locked the door. No one can walk in on us. You never work as efficiently when you're stressed. Let me help you relax, and it will all be better."

I closed my mouth around the head of his cock as my hand gently stroked the shaft, and he instantly grew hard. Jack sighed aloud with pleasure as I took in the length of him with my mouth. Those sighs turned to moans as I took him in completely, all the way to the base, deep-throating him with the workings of my mouth.

"That feels so good, Violet."

Jack panted and moaned, running his hands through my hair as I sucked him. Then, he stopped me with a gentle touch of his hand and brought me up from my knees.

"My turn," he grinned, and he lifted me up to sit on his desk. He pushed the hem of my skirt up to my waist so he could peel off my panties and spread my thighs wide.

Kissing my mouth passionately, Jack fondled my breast

under my blouse with one hand and massaged my clit with his other hand until I was wet and ready. My entire body quivered with pleasure, wanting more.

"I want you inside me," I moaned, reaching for his cock. He grabbed a condom from his wallet, tore open the package, and slid it over his length.

He pulled me to the edge of the desk and entered me with a solid thrust that took my breath away. I wrapped my legs around his waist and twined my arms around his torso, holding him to me as he fucked me passionately right there on this desk.

"I'm coming," I moaned softly, trying to keep my voice quiet so everyone in the office wouldn't hear, even though I wanted to scream it from the top of my lungs.

The pleasure was incredible as my orgasm coursed through me in flood of joy.

I let go of his chest and leaned back, bracing my palms on the hard desktop beneath me, as he pounded into me, and I struggled to stifle my cries of rapture.

As my climax subsided, Jack pulled me off the desk to a standing position and turned me around so I was facing the desk.

"Bend forward," he said, his voice husky with lust.

I bent forward at the waist so that my torso was lying flush against the desk and gripped the sides of sturdy wood surface. Jack entered me from behind with a bold thrust that pressed me hard against the desk. I had to brace myself as he fucked me powerfully.

"I'm coming again," I gasped and moaned, barely able to keep my voice down. Intense pleasure rocked through me with every thrust.

"I'm coming too," Jack said with gritted teeth. I could feel him shudder as he emptied his seed into the condom, and my body rode a wave of ecstasy as I climaxed along with him in perfect unity.

He stayed inside me for a moment, bending down to brush my hair aside and place a tender kiss on my neck. He pulled out of me, producing a handkerchief to wipe me off.

"Ah, I really needed that," Jack sighed with contentment as we both straightened our clothes and put his desk back in order.

"I could tell," I said and smiled at him. "I needed it too."

It was nice to see him looking so much happier and relaxed, and I liked knowing that it was because of me. Plus, it didn't hurt that my body was still tingling with the after-glow of my own orgasm.

"I don't know what I'd do without you." Jack pulled me into his arms for a final kiss goodbye before I had to return to work. His hand gently caressed my cheek as he attempted to smooth my hair and a moment of tenderness passed between us.

Jack and I shared an understanding and a connection beyond anything I'd ever experienced. It was scary and wonderful at the same time, and just like the sex, I wanted more.

CHAPTER 15

JACK

"*S*o, how was your day?" Violet asked with a naughty wink as she stepped into the elevator.

It was hours after our little session in my office. Everyone else had gone home. The two of us were alone together as we rode the elevator down to the parking lot.

"It was really good," I said. She smiled.

"It's a shame every day can't be that good," she said wistfully, and I felt a strain of arousal in my pants just thinking about it. "That was our last time, right?" she asked teasingly.

"We both know it won't be our last time, Violet. Why are we fighting this? We're so perfect together in bed, or anyplace else for that matter. Why don't we just agree to have a sexual relationship like we want to?"

"Well, for starters, you're my boss and I'm your EA," she said, snapping back to reality. "How would it look if we made a habit of sleeping together? There'd be allegations of favoritism and sexual harassment, the scandals would be endless, and ultimately, our happiness could seriously hurt the company."

She had a good point, but I wasn't ready to give up so

easily. Cocking my eyebrow mischievously, I smirked and said, "Not if nobody knows about it."

"You mean have a secret affair?" Violet looked shocked, but her expression quickly morphed into one of intrigue.

"Why not?" I said excitedly. "We're two consenting adults. Who we sleep with is nobody's business but our own. I say we should be able to fuck as much as we want to, and we aren't obligated to tell anybody."

"We could be discreet," Violet agreed. "I could go to your place in the evenings after work or on weekends. Nobody would need to know."

"And there wouldn't have to be any strings attached. It shouldn't affect our ability to work together. I wouldn't expect anything from you, and you wouldn't expect anything from me. Our relationship would be strictly sex and strictly for fun."

"I agree," Violet said, smiling. She was fully onboard with my plan now.

The elevator doors opened and we stepped out into the parking lot. Smiling at me sexily, Violet caressed my arm and said, "We could start tonight if you want."

"You read my mind." I leaned in to kiss her soft lips but was interrupted when her stomach suddenly growled, making mine do the same. Once again, we'd worked through lunch that day. Chuckling lightly, I said, "But first, let me take you out to dinner."

"Okay, but it's not a date," Violet said sternly, and I agreed.

"Not a date."

We passed up the pizzeria this time. Instead, I took her to a real restaurant, with cloth napkins and a maître d'. I knew Violet wasn't the kind of girl to care about how much money I spent on her, but I wanted to take her someplace special. I felt like she deserved to be pampered a little after the way she'd taken care of me that morning when I was losing my shit. It wasn't often that I needed help at work, but whenever I did, I could count on Violet to know just what I needed. She'd proven that on several occasions now, and so I wanted to show her how much I appreciated her with more than just pizza.

The waiter brought our appetizers, and I ordered a bottle of their best cabernet. Halfway through the salad, I nearly choked to death on my arugula when Violet asked, "So, why are you still a bachelor?"

I took a long swallow of wine to clear my throat and said, "I don't know. I guess I just haven't found the right girl yet."

"Oh, don't give me that old cliché," Violet said. "You're rich, handsome, charming, excellent in bed. There's a reason a man like you isn't married yet. If we're going to have an ongoing sexual relationship, I just want to know what I'm getting into."

"All right, if you must know, most women are gold diggers," I stated boldly.

"Oh, really?" Violet looked more amused than insulted as she swirled her glass of wine.

"At least, most women have been, in my own personal experience," I said, softening my tone. "When I was a kid, I was too embarrassed to bring a girl home and have her meet my drunk dad. And after I ran away, I was too busy surviving. So it wasn't until college, when I was working on my first computer app, that I had the confidence to ask a girl out. Her name was Charli. I gave her my virginity, and she stole my app and sold it for a small fortune. After that, I became a lot more wary about the women I dated, but it didn't help. Every time I let myself develop feelings for someone, she broke my heart and emptied my wallet. The more wealth I acquired, the bigger the target I became for craftier schemes. Now, it's impossible for me to trust any woman who wants to go out with me. I have to make sure she's not out to use me and take as much as she can get."

It was the first time I'd ever confessed those feelings out loud, and it was a surprising relief. I'd been building a thick wall around my heart for a long time, and it was nice to be able to confide to someone why. Still, I worried how Violet would take it. Luckily, she wasn't offended.

"That's awful, Jack. But, you know, men are no different," Violet said, and I mused how only she could manage to be both sympathetic and sassy at the same time. It made me want to kiss her from across the table.

"Oh, really?" I echoed her own response with a wry grin, and the sexual tension between us became palatable as the waiter served our entrées.

"Don't think just because you're wealthier than me that I don't know what it's like to have men use me for my money," Violet challenged, her eyes flashing sexily. "My ex-boyfriend was a deadbeat right from the start. Not only did I have to support him financially, but he had me cleaning his house and doing his laundry like I was his mother."

"That's an option?" I teased, serving her back some of her own sass to lighten the mood. "Maybe you can do a couple loads of laundry for me when we get to my place. It's really piling up."

"Forget it!" Violet teased back with mock anger. "Never again am I going to let someone take advantage of me like that. I came to LA to make a career for myself, not provide free maid service to some man. If I wanted to do that, I'd have just married Mark Hansen back in Iowa, but I value my independence too much."

"So we're just a couple of work-minded people who were spurned by the users of this world, not looking for love, just wanting to fuck and have a good time," I said. Violet giggled as she nodded in agreement. I filled both our glasses and raised mine in a toast, saying, "To great sex, no strings attached."

Violet echoed my words and we drained our glasses together.

We spent the rest of the evening laughing and sharing stories of our lives. I'd forgotten how fun it was to really get to know someone and to let her get to know me too. With Violet, there was no risk of her hurting me, since there was no romantic attachment, no commitment. We were both on the same page when it came to relationships, and I could let my guard down.

"Do you think you'll ever want to get married and have kids?" she asked me casually over dessert.

"No. After seeing what my parents went through, a family is the last thing I'd ever want," I confessed. Normally, I would evade such a question, but with Violet, I instinctively knew she was someone I could trust with the truth.

"You're not poor like your father was," Violet pointed out. "You wouldn't have the same financial struggles your parents did if you had a kid."

"Maybe not, but what if having a kid was too much for me? Maybe I'd be a shitty dad. Or worse, I could become an alcoholic under the pressure, like my father was." I shook my head and stared off into the distance. "I know what it's like to have an abusive father, and it's too much of a risk. I'd rather never have a family than put a kid through that."

"I don't think you could ever become like that." Violet took my hand in both of hers and squeezed it tenderly. I looked in her eyes for a moment and then back down at my plate.

The mood was getting far too serious, and I needed to lighten it. Turning the tables on Violet, I asked, "What about you? Do you plan to have a husband and kids one day?"

"I do," she said proudly, "but not for a while. I want to

have a career first and enjoy my independence. Sometime down the road, I'm sure I'll meet someone, get married, and eventually we'll have children."

"There's no reason you couldn't have your career and be a mother," I pointed out. "You don't have to choose one over the other."

"I know, but I saw how having kids occupied a hundred percent of my own mother's time, and the same is true for my sister, Jessica. Right now, I want to be able to focus all my attention on my career."

I nodded. "Makes sense."

"I've been thinking a lot about creating a website to sell my jewelry online. Maddie offered to help me. Don't worry, I'll still be your EA, and I'll work on my jewelry on the weekends," she said, pausing to take a sip of wine. "Right now the only baby I want is my jewelry business. But that doesn't mean I don't still enjoy a good fuck."

She smiled naughtily at me.

My cock grew instantly hard, and I wished I could take her right then. Gazing at Violet across the table, I marveled that she just might be the perfect woman for me. We were so different from one another, and yet in a lot of ways, we were the same.

She understood why Lion was so important to me, just like I knew why she'd be a huge success if she turned her hobby into a real business. And amazingly, Violet understood why I didn't trust women. She wasn't trying to change my mind or to be the one woman to finally win my heart. Everything with her was so natural, so easy.

Violet was the first person I could truly open up to and be myself with.

Not to mention she had a smoking hot body I wanted to fuck again and again.

"Come away with me this weekend," I said, totally out of

the blue. The words just tumbled out of my mouth before I even knew I was saying them.

"What?" Violet blinked in surprise at the invitation.

I was just as stunned, but as I thought about it, the idea was perfect. Work had been so stressful. I needed to relax and get away, but I didn't want to do it alone. Violet was the first woman I trusted to not go after my money. She was so fun and open with her mind and her body. We always had a good time together, and the sex was phenomenal. Why shouldn't we go away together?

"Where would we go?" Violet asked with an air of hesitation and curiosity.

"Not far. I have a beach house a couple hours' drive outside the city. Your friend Stuart sold it to me. It's the perfect place to unwind after all the long hours we've been putting in at work."

"Won't going away together break our new pact of no strings attached?"

She was right. *Logically*, I knew she was right. If Violet and I wanted to keep our relationship strictly sexual and not develop feelings for each other, a weekend away together was a big mistake. But I wasn't listening to my brain. I was listening to the organs below my neck, like my heart and my rock-hard cock, and they both had other ideas.

I reached across the table and squeezed her hand.

"Don't worry," I said. "This will be the perfect way to seal the pact. It'll be a weekend of pure fun – and plenty of sex, of course. No strings attached, I promise."

CHAPTER 16

VIOLET

"*R*ise and shine, beautiful."

I opened my eyes to see Jack entering the room with a wooden tray in his hands.

"Well, this is a nice way to start the day." I beamed as he set the tray on my lap. He'd made a spinach frittata with fresh berries and cream on the side. My eyes flew open wide as I took the first bite of the frittata. "This is delicious! I never would have guessed you could cook like this."

"It's just a little hobby I picked up over the years," he said. "When you grow up with little to no money for food, you have to learn how to be creative with whatever odd ingredients you receive in the donation boxes. Once I started making some money, I discovered a whole world of groceries from the markets and started watching those cooking shows on YouTube."

"You really are a Jack of all trades," I teased before shoveling more in my mouth. "This is truly delicious. Maybe you missed your calling as a professional chef."

"Nah," Jack waved off the compliment as he settled beside me in his heavenly king-sized bed. "Cooking is for fun, but my true passion will always lie in computer tech. I can spend hours working on something and not even realize any time has gone by. And running this company is even more exhilarating. When business is doing well, it makes me feel alive. It's the same feeling you get when you're working on your jewelry."

"What are you talking about?" I stared at him in disbelief. I didn't realize anyone knew the joy my craft gave me. I considered it something intimate I did just for me. How did he know how I felt inside?

"Last night, when you sat down with your jewelry and started making those little heart bracelets, you were lost in another world," Jack explained with an air of amusement. "I had to call your name three times to get your attention."

I blushed. "Sorry I was so spaced out."

I suddenly felt like the worst person on the planet. The previous afternoon he'd brought me to his beautiful, luxurious beach house, and I'd spent half the evening making jewelry.

"No big deal," he said, leaning in to give me a kiss.

"I didn't mean to ignore you."

"No, it was nice seeing you so wrapped up doing what you love. I just sat there watching you, and you didn't even realize it. A peace had come over you, and you looked so serene."

"So, you're like a creepy stalker?" I teased him.

"Only for you." Jack grinned, and he pushed the breakfast tray away to kiss me. I melted in his arms.

AFTER AN INTENSE QUICKIE in the shower, we got dressed for the beach. It was the first time I'd ever seen Jack in shorts and a T-shirt. It suited him. His killer abs and pectoral muscles could be seen clearly beneath the thin cotton fabric of his designer shirt, and I wanted to run my hands over his strong chest.

I put on a summer dress, not realizing the floral pattern was accidentally the same shades of blue and green that Jack was wearing. When I caught a glimpse of us reflected in the living room mirror, I was stunned to realize we looked like a real-life couple – one of those cutesy ones who always dressed alike.

I ran into the bedroom and quickly rummaged through my suitcase desperately looking for something else I could change into that wouldn't scream, "We're a couple!" But I'd only packed a few things for the weekend, and this dress was pretty much my only option.

I was about to fly into a panic when the realization slowly dawned me. Here at the beach, it didn't matter if we looked like we were together. This wasn't the office where we needed to hide our friends-with-benefits arrangement. It wasn't even LA. There was no risk we'd be seen by someone we knew when we went out to dinner.

Jack's scenic beach house was far enough away from the city where we both lived and worked that it was like being in a different land. We were finally free to display our attraction for each other openly. We could hold hands and even kiss in public if we wanted to. It seemed the beach was a paradise for more reasons than one.

I emerged from the bedroom to find Jack had packed a picnic for two. He loaded the food into a backpack, which he slung over his shoulder with one easy movement. I liked the way his shoulder muscles flexed as he did it, and I felt my nipples tingle beneath my dress, longing for his touch.

"You look ready for a hike. Am I dressed appropriately?" I worried, looking down at my sundress and flat sandals, but Jack just grinned at me.

"Don't change a thing. You look perfect." He took me by the hand and led me outside where two shiny bicycles were waiting.

"I haven't ridden a bike since I was a kid," I said with surprise.

"I hardly have either," Jack admitted, "but I figured this is the perfect weekend for doing all the things that make life worth living. Otherwise, what are we working for all the time?"

I was a little uncertain on the bike at first, but it didn't take me long to get used to it. Soon I was coasting down the bike path with the sun on my face, smiling and laughing like a schoolgirl.

We skidded to a stop at the end of the path, and I was thrilled to discover we were right on the beach. I helped Jack secure the bikes to a metal rack and then turned to face the glorious ocean waves lapping up on the sandy shore. It was breathtaking!

Jack stripped off his shirt to reveal his sexy chest, and I followed suit, peeling off my dress to show off the bikini I'd brought for the trip. Looking out at all the skinny beach bodies lying in the sand across the beach, I suddenly felt self-conscious in the little swimsuit. But all I had to do was see the way Jack was staring at me, and I knew I had nothing to worry about.

"You look gorgeous," he breathed with dilated eyes. Then he looked out at the waves and grinned with boyish glee. Arching his left brow, he said, "Wanna race?"

"I don't know. What about our stuff?" I said with a worried frown.

Jack turned and looked at our clothes hanging on the handles of our bicycles, saying, "Our stuff will be fine. And if someone steals it, I'll buy you new clothes."

And when he turned back to look at me, I was already

halfway down the beach, running toward the water as fast as I could, kicking up sand behind me.

"No fair! You cheated!" Jack laughed, and I squealed as I heard him running toward me, quickly gaining. I reached the edge of the water just moments before him. I celebrated my victory, jumping in the surf with my arms in the air and the water splashing around me.

Suddenly, my victory dance was cut short when Jack tackled me playfully, and we fell into an oncoming wave with a splash, laughing all the while. The cold water took my breath away, and I lunged at Jack, dragging him into the water with me as the next wave came, soaking us both.

We were like a couple of teenagers, playing in the water, splashing and wrestling in the waves one moment, kissing each other the next. He tasted like salt and coconut oil, and I wished the beach were a private one so we could have sex right there in the water.

We finally collapsed on the sandy beach, exhausted and happy, and I saw two young children playing nearby.

"Let's build a sandcastle!" I said to Jack, and his deep blue eyes instantly lit up.

Using only our hands and some small pieces of drift-wood, we piled up a huge mound of sand and then carefully sculpted it with our fingers until it formed into a beautiful, sprawling castle. Jack concentrated as he carved detailed designs in the sand. People stopped to look, impressed.

"Where did you learn how to sculpt sand like that?" I asked as we admired our work.

"I'm a man of many talents," Jack said jokingly. He folded his hands behind his head as he stretched out on the sand to rest.

"You're modest, too," I laughed as I stretched out beside him.

But it was true – he did have many talents. I lay beside

him, marveling at what an amazing man he was. He stroked my hair, and we fell asleep for a short nap in the warm sun.

Later that day, we went for a stroll along the surf, holding hands as we searched for seashells. Back at the house, I helped him cook a gourmet dinner, and then we had incredible sex all night long until we finally fell asleep just as the sun was rising over the horizon.

On Sunday, we slept till noon and then scarfed down brunch. It was the last day of what had been a perfect weekend, and we both hated to return to LA that night. After we ate, we ran back to bed for more sex, giggling and wrestling under the sheets like horny teenagers. Our appetites for each other were insatiable, and every time I thought sex with Jack couldn't possibly get any better, he proved me wrong with intense orgasms that seemed to last forever.

After the car was packed and it was almost time to leave, Jack took me back to the beach for a final walk on the sand as the waves crashed nearby.

"Look!" he said, coming to a sudden stop. "It's a conch shell."

He pointed at the rare shell bobbing out at some distance in the water.

"Beautiful," I said.

"I'm going to get it for you," he said, a grin lighting up his face.

With one quick movement, he removed his shirt and tossed it on the sand.

"No, Jack, you don't have to do that," I said.

He ran out toward the breaking waves.

"Don't! The tide is too high right now!" I cried out, but I was too late. He dove under a wave and swam from the shore, covering the distance to the shell quickly.

I shielded my eyes as I watched him swim away from me, the waves tossing him around. But he was a powerful swimmer, and he headed straight toward the shell. Just before he reached it, a wave plunged the shell under the surface, and he dove below the water after it.

"Oh, Jack, you're going to give me a heart attack," I muttered to myself as he disappeared in the surf.

He was under the water for what felt like forever, and I bit my lip in suspense. Finally, he emerged, gasping for air, and turned back toward the shore. He swam out of the waves and walked up to me on the beach, water dripping from his sexy, muscular body.

"For you, so you can remember this weekend," he said breathlessly. He placed the large pink shell in my hands and kissed my lips tenderly.

"Thank you, Jack. I love it!" I said, and I couldn't keep my emotions from strangling my voice. Unbidden, tears sprang to my eyes, and I had to force them back.

"What's wrong?" He caressed my cheek, looking worried.

"It's nothing." I shrugged and tried to laugh it off. "It's just that no one has ever given me anything like this before. Nathan was beyond useless, and Mark only wanted to talk about farming," I joked, trying to keep the mood light. "I guess I'm not used to anyone making me feel special like this."

"Well, get used to it. You deserve to know what a fantastic woman you are," Jack said earnestly. I couldn't help but throw myself at him and kiss him again.

We made love one last time in the shadows of the setting sun, hidden behind a range of rocks on a secluded part of the beach as the sky grew dark. It was the perfect way to end the magical weekend, but I felt a lot sadder to be going home than I ever imagined I would.

On the car ride home, I cranked up some Led Zeppelin. I sang along with Jack, hoping to drown out my disappointment that my time together with him was over. I hadn't expected it would be so hard to say goodbye after just one weekend together – and it wasn't really goodbye, since I'd see him tomorrow at work. But tomorrow we'd have to pretend again.

We had grown incredibly close in a short period of time.

Jack was so tender and sweet. The scars of his youth ran deep, and the troubles with women trying to scam him for his money only exacerbated his pain. Now that I knew the real story of his painful past, it was understandable why he would build a wall around his heart.

I was surprised by just how disappointed I felt when Jack first revealed to me that he didn't want to have children. After all, it wasn't like I was planning to marry him and have his babies. Motherhood wasn't something I wanted until much further down the road, although I'd have been a liar if I'd said I didn't think Jack would make a good husband and father – much better than he himself thought he would make. But that was just a silly fantasy. We weren't in a romantic relationship. We were just together for the sex, nothing serious or long-term.

So what if we had a deep connection and were able to share the most intimate details of our lives with one another? It didn't matter that we had such great chemistry, both in and out of bed. None of it meant anything serious.

And the fact that he dove into the ocean at high tide to collect a conch shell for me – and gave it to me to remember him by – well, that didn't mean anything either, did it?

I couldn't *let* it mean anything to me. That was part of our agreement.

More importantly, it didn't mean anything to him. The realization made a lump form in my throat as he drove us through the city.

Jack pulled his car to a stop in front of my apartment and gallantly walked me to my door.

"Thanks for a wonderful weekend." I smiled up at him, clutching the conch shell to my chest.

"You're the one who made it wonderful." Jack gazed into my eyes, his own blue ones like two liquid pools staring directly into my soul. My heart fluttered as he cupped my face and drew me to him in a soft and tender kiss. He pulled away slowly, as if he didn't want to say goodbye any more than I did.

Softly he whispered, "I'll see you at work. Sweet dreams."

Then, he was gone.

That night, I lay in bed for a long time, unable to sleep.

Was I falling for Jack McCann, the man who had started off as the worst boss in the world and had slowly turned into a Prince Charming?

As I counted down the minutes until I could be in his arms again, I knew that I was. The question was, could Jack be falling for me too?

The answer was impossible to know, but as I stared at the shell he had given me in the moonlight, I hoped with all my heart that he was.

CHAPTER 17

JACK

"Good morning, Kate. How's my favorite receptionist today?" I walked into the office carrying a huge box of donuts in my arms and held it out to her.

"I'm well. Thank you, Mr. McCann." Kate looked pleasantly taken aback as she plucked a chocolate sprinkled donut from the box with a smile.

"You're welcome, and call me Jack," I insisted for the hundredth time, even though I knew she'd never change.

I waltzed through the office, singing my favorite upbeat rock song – only slightly off-key.

"Donut, Maddie? Good job on the Morris account, by the way. Donut, Floyd? Pass the box on down the aisle."

"Someone had a good weekend," Grayson said, walking into the office and pouring himself a coffee.

"I had a great weekend." I grinned as I handed him the pastry I had saved wrapped in paper. "Bear claw? I know they're your favorite."

"Thanks. Don't mind if I do," Grayson said, and he followed me into my office. He sat in the chair across from my desk and put my feet up with ease. "So, what's she like in bed?"

"Who?" I asked, my heart pounding in my chest like a fucking drum. I was playing dumb, but it was clear he'd found out.

How did Grayson know I'd slept with Violet? I'd thought taking her to the beach house was the perfect hideaway. I guess I should have known keeping our affair secret wouldn't be that easy.

"Don't bullshit me," Grayson said, polishing off his bear claw in three easy bites. I swear, the guy was like a garbage disposal. Grayson put his feet on the floor and bore his eyes into my soul, like a master interrogator. "You've been grouching around here for months, biting everyone's head off over the stupidest shit, and now today you're practically breaking out in song and dance. So confess. Who's the girl?"

"I just had a relaxing weekend, that's all." I shrugged like it was no big deal, while inside I was sighing with relief that he didn't really know I was sleeping with Violet after all.

We'd agreed from the beginning of Lion, Inc., that sleeping with employees was completely off limits. And now I'd broken our cardinal rule – multiple times this past weekend alone.

Trying to act cool, I put my hands behind my head and kicked back in my chair, saying, "I went out to my new beach house. It was just what I needed. A little sun, a little surf. I feel like a new man."

"Yeah, bullshit." Grayson laughed. "Fine, keep your secret, don't tell me who she is or what she looks like, but at least tell me where you met her."

"Nowhere," I insisted. "There's no secret woman, Grayson."

"Well, I know you didn't meet her at any of the bars we used to hang out at." Grayson pouted childishly. "When was the last time you went out with me on a Friday night to the clubs? We used to go every week. Now, I'm dying out there alone without my wingman!"

"I'm sorry, buddy. Maybe next time." Rising to my feet, I clasped his shoulder sympathetically as a ruse to guide him out of his chair and shepherd him out of my office. I wasn't about to tell him that ever since I met Violet, I no longer had interest in picking up women at the bars anymore.

"I'll hold you to that promise," Grayson said. He looked like a hungry wolf. I actually felt bad for the guy.

As Grayson left, I caught sight of a delivery boy bringing in a huge bouquet of tropical flowers, full of passion flowers, birds of paradise, jasmine, and hibiscus.

Kate directed the delivery boy to Violet's desk, and she gasped with surprise as he set them down before her. She looked so stunning when she smiled with her eyes like that, it sent thrills through me to know I was the one who had made her feel that way.

"That's practically the entire rainforest. Who are they from?" Maddie cried out excitedly.

"I don't know," Violet stammered.

I could tell she wanted to look in my direction, but she restrained herself. Instead, she reached for the card and read it. She quickly folded the card and stuffed it in her pocket, saying lamely, "They're for my birthday."

"It's not your birthday," Maddie was quick to point out.

"Well, what can I say? Someone made a mistake."

I wiped a smile from my face. Violet was such a bad liar. It was painful to watch and yet utterly adorable. I decided I'd better go rescue her before her lies got any worse.

Striding from my office, I threw her a stern look and said, "Those are nice flowers, but I believe you have work to do. Maddie, you do too."

As Maddie rushed back to her computer, Violet looked

at me and silently mouthed the words 'Thank you.' I couldn't tell if she meant for the flowers or chasing Maddie off, but it didn't really matter. I'd seen the look on her face when she got the delivery, and it was everything I'd hoped it would be.

IT WAS a trend that continued over the next weeks. I loved pampering her, though most of the time I was more discreet than having flowers delivered at the office.

Violet was never greedy or selfish or out to take me for as much as she could get. Whenever I gave her a gift or took her out somewhere, she was truly amazed and appreciative, which made me want to give her all the more.

Nobody deserved to be pampered more than her, and I liked doing it. My only worry was finding a gift that would top the last one. It didn't have to always be expensive. Sometimes the best gifts were the ones that were the most sentimental, like the special corn cakes I had shipped from a bakery in Iowa.

"I used to eat this all the time when I was a kid!" Violet's eyes danced with joy as she sampled them. "They were my favorite treat growing up. I haven't had any in years!"

"I remember you said something about them the last time we were at the beach house," I said.

Sometimes, I wondered if I was falling for her, but I quickly shook off the ridiculous idea. Our relationship was strictly sexual, no strings attached. It was only natural that I would want to spoil the woman I had such great sex with, that's all. Nothing more... even if I wanted to spend every moment with her during the day. And dreamed about her at night.

Soon, a month had passed, and I wanted to give Violet

something that would blow her away. It needed to be lavish enough to display how much she meant to me.

"Happy casual Friday." Violet breezed into my office looking more beautiful than ever in a floral sundress that flowed around her like the petals of a rose. She looked so cute in those, even more than the blazers and skirts that were her regular office attire, that I decided to institute casual Friday as an excuse to see her in them more often.

Knowing I liked the dresses, Violet gave me a little flirty twirl before sitting on the edge of my desk to taunt me with her tan legs.

"Happy one-month anniversary." I grinned, and Violet drew in her breath with surprise.

"Has it really been a month since we started our pact?" she asked.

It disappointed me to hear her call it that. Pact sounded so cold and unromantic, but then again, that's what we agreed to. Just sex, no strings attached. Still, that didn't mean I couldn't mark the passage of time with something special.

Trying to play it off casually, I said, "I have to go down the coast to one of Morris's hotels to personally check on some things. Want to go with me?"

"That sounds nice, but I have a lot of work I need to finish here before the weekend," Violet said. She surprised me by turning me down. Shit!

"I could really use the help of my assistant. Your other work can wait. Our biggest client needs to take priority," I said, trying to be authoritative and charming at the same time. "Besides, I'm the boss. Who else is going to complain if your work isn't done?"

"Well, when you put it that way, let's go!" Violet beamed. Her smile always melted me like the flame of a candle. It was so warm and bright, it drew me to her like a moth.

We made out in the elevator all the way down to the

parking garage, and were almost caught by one of the programmers walking in.

"That was close!" Violet giggled as she buried her face in her hands after he'd gone.

"That's why we're going far away," I said, and she laughed happily at my joke. I loved hearing the sound of her laughter. It was so easy and free, just like her smile. Just being near her lifted my heart and made everything easier. With Violet, I didn't have to be guarded or tough. I could just relax and be my true self.

I wondered if she felt the same way about me. Not that I had feelings for her. I just enjoyed her company, that was all.

I cranked up the tunes in my car. We raced along the coast, down winding roads and long straightaways. Violet had quickly become a fan of classic rock, and we sang along to "More Than a Feeling" by Boston with our hands intertwined.

We pulled to a stop in front of Vista del Mar, the premier luxury hotel for the Vista Hotel chain. I made a show of meeting with the manager and verifying that our cybersecurity service was working well and there weren't any issues, and then he revealed the true reason for our visit.

"So, your room is ready for check-in. Would you like to see it now?" the manager asked, and I could feel Violet's feisty stare boring into the back of my head.

"I thought you said this was a work trip?" she whispered in my ear on the elevator ride up to the penthouse.

"It was. I worked. Now I'm done, so I might as well enjoy the weekend in their best suite."

"I should have known you were up to something." Violet pretended to be mad, but she couldn't hide the smile tugging at the corner of her lips.

"The suite comes with a private hot tub, fully stocked bar,

and all the other amenities," the bellhop said as he gave us a quick tour. "Please let me know if you need anything else."

I handed him a generous tip as he left and then turned to find Violet spinning in a big circle in the middle of the grand suite with her arms spread wide and her head thrown back while her sundress fanned out around her.

"This suite is amazing," she sang out. Then she ran toward the bed, jumped into the air, and flung herself on the giant California-king bed like a joyous child.

"Careful," I called out, just as she landed next to the hard little box I'd had the staff place there for me when we first arrived.

"What's this?" Violet picked up the small white gift box and held it up, staring at it quizzically.

"I don't know," I shrugged with a smile. "I guess you'd better open it to find out."

"You didn't need to get me anything." Violet's beautiful face flushed with embarrassment.

"I know I didn't have to, but I like buying you little gifts of appreciation. Nobody deserves it more than you."

"Well, you shouldn't have," Violet chastised. Tugging at the bow, she untied the silk ribbon and slowly opened the lid of the white box to reveal a black velvet box within from an exclusive jewelry designer in Beverly Hills.

I watched with eager anticipation as she gently lifted the lid of the black box with trembling hands and then gasped at what she found within.

"Are you serious?" Violet whispered with awe as she stared at the piece I'd had specially made just for her.

"Of course," I said.

"It looks like a violet," she gasped, as her index finger delicately stroked the flower-shaped pendant on a gold necklace chain. The petals of the flower were made of amethyst with a diamond in the center.

"Let me help you put it on." I stepped up behind her and clasped the chain around her delicate neck.

"It's gorgeous, but… it's too much, Jack," she objected, trying to stop me, but the clasp was already closed in place.

"Actually, it's not enough," I insisted, and I guided her to a mirror so she could see for herself how the pendant was meant to be hers. "You give so much to me every day, and you don't even know it. I just want to try to give a little token to show you how much I value you. Please let me."

She stood there in awe, staring at her reflection in the mirror, gazing at the costly jeweled pendant with tears in her eyes. My heart swelled to be able to give her such joy.

Violet turned to face me and whispered, "Thank you. I – I don't know what to say."

"Don't say anything," I said, and I pulled her into my arms and kissed her passionately. She melted into my embrace, giving herself over to the heat of moment, and I heard a soft sigh escape her throat.

I lifted her into my arms and carried her to the bed. I laid her right in the center of the soft mattress and climbed onto the bed beside her.

Violet's sundress had a row of delicate pearl buttons down the front, and I took my time unfastening them one by one in a trail down her body. It was like unwrapping a present of my own, and I delighted in kissing every inch of her body as it was revealed.

Soon we were both naked, and I marveled at how incredibly gorgeous her body was as she stretched out across the bed before me. Her breasts were two perfectly round globes that filled my hands, and I watched as she arched her back, pushing them towards my mouth as I suckled and kissed them all over. Her nipples became two hard, dark nubs, and I rolled them between my finger and thumb each in turn, while I kissed the other, alternating back and forth.

She reached down with her hand and found my manhood, stroking me into full hardness. When she positioned herself to take my hard cock into her hot, wet mouth, I had to bite my tongue to keep from coming right then, it felt so fucking good. I positioned myself so my face was between her thighs, so we could pleasure each other with our mouths together at the same time.

My tongue luxuriated in Violet's most intimate folds, lapping and flicking, kissing and suckling, until Violet was delirious with pleasure beneath my touch. It thrilled me to know that I was the one making her feel so good.

Next, I took my index finger and slid it into her tight, wet slit, and she raised her hips, wanting more. I added a second finger and then a third, fucking her with them while I pleasured her clit with my tongue in just the way she liked best. Soon, she was climaxing beneath my touch. Her face contorted in the sweet bliss of orgasm as her body writhed with ecstasy.

In that moment, I slipped on a condom and entered her, plunging my rock-hard cock deep into her quivering tight slit. She was so wet, I penetrated her all the way to my balls with one easy thrust, and I could feel the walls of her pussy pulsing around my dick, welcoming me inside her.

Slowly, I began to thrust in and out as far as I could go. She felt so fucking good, it took all my willpower not to climax, but I wanted to draw out the pleasure and make it last.

Violet wrapped her arms around my torso, drawing me to her so that her tits rested against my naked chest as she took my mouth with hers in a deep kiss. Her legs wrapped around my waist, and I put my hands under her sweet round ass, raising her up and changing the angle of her hips.

"Fuck me harder," Violet moaned aloud, and I let myself go, pumping into her as hard and fast as I could, driving her to orgasm for the second time. I could see the jewels of her necklace glittering as the pendant danced between her tits, and she tossed her head back in the throes of rapture.

I felt my own orgasm coming, and I tried to stop it, but I couldn't hold back any longer. It was here, and I gasped for breath as my body exploded with the most intense pleasure a human being could experience. I could feel Violet's body undulating as her muscles spasmed around me, and I knew she was climaxing along with me in beautiful perfect symmetry, our two bodies becoming one. The glorious moment lasted for an eternity until we were both utterly spent and I collapsed onto the bed beside her.

"That was amazing," I whispered into her hair as she cuddled against my sweaty chest and we held each other close.

She murmured in agreement, already dozing off.

She fell asleep in my arms as I stroked her long chestnut mane, and I realized in that moment that she was much more to me than just an employee, and more than a fuck buddy.

Whatever was happening between us was about much more than just sex to me.

Only I could never tell Violet, because then I would lose her.

She'd made it clear countless times that she didn't want any attachment. But for me, it was already forming, and there was nothing I could do to stop it.

CHAPTER 18

VIOLET

"*H*ey stranger, long time no see," Stuart teased as I let myself into our apartment early Monday morning to grab some clothes. "I haven't seen you in so long, I wasn't sure if you still lived here or not."

"Of course I do, and here's this month's rent to prove it, plus some interest on all the times I was late and you covered for me." I handed him an envelope with a check I retrieved from my bag, but he didn't take it. He just stared at my neck with his mouth open wide.

"Look at that spectacular necklace! I've never seen gemstones sparkle so bright. It's no wonder you've been spending nearly every night for the past month at Lover Boy's place. With rocks like those weighing you down, I'd be amazed if you have the strength to get out of bed."

"Hardy har, Stuart." I pulled my jacket around me tighter, trying to hide the embarrassingly extravagant pendant. "I am not sleeping with Jack so he'll buy me jewelry. I'm with him because I enjoy his company and the sex is the best I've ever had. I'm not in it to see how much I can get out of him. Our relationship is supposed to be no strings attached, and

honestly, this gift is way too expensive for a casual relationship."

"Oh, sweetie, if you don't want a rich, handsome
boyfriend who buys you extravagant gifts, please give him to
me. I'll take him with strings or without, however he wants
me." Stuart mimed tying a ribbon around himself in a big
bow, and I couldn't help but laugh.

"Shut up and take your rent money." I smacked him playfully with the envelope before handing it to him. "I just
stopped by to change clothes before work. If I show up
Monday mornings in the same outfit I was wearing Friday
night, my coworkers are bound to get suspicious. I think
Maddie already is."

"Don't worry, sweetie, with jewels like those around your
neck, nobody will notice what you're wearing."

"You're right," I said, burying my face in my hands. "It's
way too much, but you should have seen the look on Jack's
face when he gave it to me. He was so excited to put it
around my neck. If I don't wear it to work today, the disappointment will kill him. On the other hand, if I do wear it,
everyone at work is going to wonder where I got something
so extravagant, and you've seen me try to lie! I'm terrible
at it!"

"Then tell the truth. Honesty is the best policy," Stuart
said.

"Are you crazy? I can't tell my coworkers I'm dating the
boss!" I cried out.

"I meant to be honest with *him*, not to announce your
affair in a company-wide memo. Jack needs to know the
truth about how you feel. It's the only way this relationship is
going to work."

"But we're not in a relationship. This is just sex, no strings
attached," I insisted. I could tell from the dramatic roll of
Stuart's eyes that he didn't believe me, but I didn't have the

time to argue with him about it unless I wanted to be late for work.

I glanced at the clock and ran into my room praying it wasn't already too late for me to get there on time, but none of my work clothes were clean. I hadn't been home long enough to do any laundry. I found my most conservative summer dress and slipped it on along with a pair of simple flats, and then I pulled my hair into a quick ponytail and ran out the door.

"Am I on time?" I asked breathlessly, as I stepped off the elevator onto the floor dedicated to Lion, Inc.

"You are," Maddie assured me. Over the weekend, her hair had turned from fuchsia to a vivid lavender. She fiddled with her matching lavender glasses and said, "I must say, I like the new look. That dress is adorable, but the necklace is a bit much."

"I know." My hands flew to cover the pendant before I could stop them. "It was a gift from a friend. I feel a little weird wearing it, but I don't want to hurt his feelings."

"*His* feelings," Maddie echoed. Then she gave a knowing smile and said, "You've got a boyfriend."

"Not a boyfriend. We have a lot of great sex, but we're not in a relationship. We both agreed, there would be nothing romantic between us."

"Except for expensive gifts of giant pendants covered in jewels?" Maddie peered over the rim of her lavender glasses, analyzing the clarity of the gemstones.

"I know, you're right. It's way too much, but I don't know what to do!" I moaned miserably. "How do I tell him the necklace is over the top without utterly crushing his feelings?"

"Jack's a pretty understanding guy, and very practical. He wouldn't want you to wear something you don't feel comfortable in just to please him," Maddie said. My jaw dropped with a gasp.

"I didn't say it was Jack. Why would he give me jewelry?" My laughter sounded painfully fake, even to my own ears.

"Please." Maddie rolled her eyes just like Stuart had done, only her glasses magnified the gesture, which somehow made it even worse. She said, "I have a photographic memory. I've been watching you two flirt and make googly eyes at each other for weeks. Those little meetings you have with his office door locked and the shades drawn aren't fooling anyone."

"Oh, no! Does everyone know?" I turned bright red with humiliation, looking around the office with darting eyes.

"I can't speak for anyone else, but I've known ever since that bouquet arrived and you practically eye-fucked him across the office," Maddie said, and I just wanted to bury my face in my hands and die. Maddie said brightly, "I wouldn't worry. If anyone does know, I doubt they would care. I'm just thankful to see the boss is finally happy and with a woman who is kind and deserves him. For a while, his bark was as bad as his byte. Get it? Byte!"

Maddie laughed merrily at her own joke, and even though I'd heard similar jokes a few dozen times already, she made me feel better.

Jack was a reasonable man. He wouldn't want me to do something I wasn't comfortable doing just for the sake of his ego. For a self-made millionaire, he was incredibly generous and unassuming. He never used his acts of charity as a way to promote his image or flaunt his wealth. He gave to others quietly, simply because he knew it was the right thing to do.

I swiftly took off the pendant before anyone else could see it and subtly stuffed it in my pocket. When Jack called me into his office, he looked disappointed I wasn't wearing the necklace.

I closed the door and asked him, "Can we have dinner tonight after work? There's something we need to talk about."

"What is it?" Jack asked with a flash of concern in his deep blue eyes.

"It's nothing urgent. We can discuss it tonight," I said gently, but Jack wasn't soothed.

"No, if you're going to end things between us, say it now. Don't leave me in suspense," he said.

"No, it's nothing like that," I said, surprised and touched that he would have such a strong reaction to the idea. "I want to keep our pact just as it is. I only wanted to explain why I wasn't wearing the pendant necklace you gave me."

"Oh, is that all?" Jack sank back in his chair, the color returning to his flesh as his panic alleviated.

"Yes, absolutely." I sat down in the chair across from his desk and held his hands in mine to give him added reassurance that everything was all right between us.

"Well, you might as well tell me now," he said, and I realized he was right.

Taking in a deep breath for courage, I pulled the jeweled violet pendant from my pocket and set it carefully on his desk. Gazing into his eyes, I said softly, "I want you to take this back."

"It was a gift. I had it made special just for you," Jack said in earnest, and I felt like a complete bitch. Still, my two closest friends had both told me the same thing: be honest with him. I knew I had to be brutally so.

"It's not me. I like jewelry to be simple and subtle, like the unassuming pieces I make. This pendant, while stunningly gorgeous, is way too extravagant for an Iowa girl like me. I feel awkward and out of place wearing it. Like I'm pretending to be someone I'm not."

"Well, that wasn't my intention when I gave it to you."

Jack looked slightly wounded, but he was taking it much more in stride than I feared he would. Suddenly, he brightened, and said, "Why don't we go to the jewelers together? They have lots of gemstones to choose from. We can trade that piece in for something you like better."

"Thank you, but I don't think I'd feel comfortable wearing any gemstones at all, especially when I have debts I'm trying to pay off."

"You're in debt?" Jack asked with genuine concern in his voice.

"My ex, Nathan, maxed out all my credit cards. I was able to get a lot of debt reduced by making arrangements with the collection agencies, but until I have them paid off, I'd feel like a hypocrite to be walking around wearing lavish gemstones."

"I get it." Jack smiled at me, that sexy grin that always melted my heart. "Nobody knows better than me what it's like to owe money to collection agencies. The moment I ever had anything nice given to me, my father would pawn it to pay the bills. I won't put you in that awkward position, but I do still want to give you something."

"I've told you before, you don't have to give me anything." I giggled with an exasperated sigh, knowing it was useless trying to get him to stop being generous.

"Nothing frivolous this time, I promise," Jack held up his hand in a solemn vow. "I want to give you a monthly bonus as part of your salary."

"Are you serious?" I could hardly believe it when he told me the amount. This could allow me to pay the debtors off in a fraction of the time.

"I am," Jack said, and I had to bite my lip to keep from crying. He squeezed my hands and said, "You bring in more clients than a lot of my sales associates. The only reason we got the Morris account was because of your brilliant marketing plan. You work long hours without complaint.

You do more for this company than most, and you deserve to be compensated. So, starting this coming payday, expect a bonus on your paycheck to reflect all the extra hard work you do."

"Will Grayson be okay with this?" I hesitated. It was almost too good to be true.

"Sure," Jack insisted, and I couldn't help but fly into his arms.

He squeezed my ass sensuously and nibbled my ear, whispering, "What do you say we cut out of here early and drive down to beach house to celebrate?"

Shaking my head, I grinned and said, "The coast is too far. What do you say we drive straight to your house here in LA? I don't want to wait any longer than necessary to fuck you."

CHAPTER 19

JACK

"Take care of things for me, will you?" I called out to Grayson urgently. "I'm going home!"

Before he could stop me, I raced down to the elevator where Violet was already waiting for me. My foot pressed hard on the gas pedal as I raced the Porsche home to my estate, and Violet and I were already half naked by the time we reached the foyer.

We left all our clothes in a trail behind us on the floor leading from the front door to the master bedroom, where Violet and I ravaged each other in a fever of lust.

I'd never been so scared as when I thought she was ending our relationship, even if it was supposed to be just a sexual one. I realized now I was already in too deep. I'd fallen for her and there was no more denying it.

When she suggested leaving work early and coming to my house to fuck, my cock sprang to full attention, eager to seal our renewed relationship in the ultimate physical manifestation of my feelings for her.

As soon as we made it to the bedroom, I carried her to the bed and devoted myself to pleasuring every inch of her naked body with my hands and mouth. I started with her toes, massaging her feet as I whispered sweet nothings to her. Then I worked my way up her tan, supple legs, kissing a trail all the way to the sweet triangle of her sex, hidden between her thighs.

My hands stretched up to massage her firm, round tits as I fucked her with my mouth in just the way I'd learned she liked best. I took her right to the brink of orgasm and then paused, right when she was ready to fall into ecstasy.

"Don't stop!" she panted, desperate for the release of climax.

But I knew she'd have a more powerful orgasm if I brought her to the edge now then pushed her into release a bit later. I grinned at her as I rolled a condom over my cock.

Lying down on my back in the middle of the bed, I guided her to mount me and said, "It's your turn to set the pace. I'll fuck you as fast or as slow as you want. Today, you're the one in charge."

She was hesitant at first, gliding her hot, tight, wet pussy slowly up and down the length of my cock. I held her tits in my hands, playfully letting my thumbs flick across her nipples as she fucked me.

Soon, she gained confidence and began thrusting harder and faster, her breathing matching pace as she panted with pleasure.

"That's it, baby. I want you to come on my cock," I encouraged, and she let herself go. Throwing back her head in ecstasy, she braced her hands against my strong chest, and fucked me with wild abandon, gasping and moaning, as she cried out my name.

I felt myself about to pop, and I grabbed her torso and held her to me, pressing her round tits against my chest. Wrapped in each other's arms, we rolled over on the bed, so now I was on top.

I kissed her lips passionately, thrusting in and out of her as slowly as I could manage to hold myself back, trying to draw out her pleasure. Violet's orgasm just kept going as she undulated and thrust against me, delirious with carnal bliss.

She grabbed my ass and squeezed, holding me to her, and cried out, "I want to feel you come inside me."

It was all the encouragement I needed. My ability to hold back was destroyed, and I thrust powerfully within her, driving deeper than I ever knew I could.

I could feel Violet's body seize in the sweet agony of orgasm, and I knew she and I were climaxing together, two bodies meshed into one in perfect unity. I called out her name as I surrendered into bliss.

Finally, we collapsed onto the mattress, sweating and panting, and unable to stop smiling. She fell asleep in my arms, and I just held her, stroking her long chestnut hair back away from her blissful face, and caressing her arm. She looked like an angel, and I didn't want to stop gazing at her.

Violet opened her eyes and caught me staring at her.

"Don't you ever sleep?" Violet teased as she stretched awake.

"I didn't want to miss a single moment of our time together," I said. Saying it aloud sounded so corny, but that didn't make it any less true. I wanted to cherish every moment I could with Violet.

Violet reached out with her delicate hand and placed it on my face, caressing my rough cheek. With smiling eyes, she said, "Well, in that case, let's make the most of this moment right now."

Then she pulled my mouth to hers and kissed me with fiery passion. We made love again and then slept for a bit, and then woke and did it all over again in the moonlight.

No matter how many times we climaxed together, I still wanted more. And so did she. There was no satisfying our appetites for each other. It was almost a disappointment when the sun rose and I knew I'd have to leave the cozy nest we'd made in my bed so I could work, until I remembered we'd still get to spend the whole day together at the office.

"Wake up, sleeping beauty," I said happily, as I nibbled her ear to gently wake her. "It's going to be a great day, and we have a lot to do."

Every day was great since Violet had come into my life, and I was happier than I ever knew I could be.

My only regret was that we couldn't be together till death do us part, but she'd made it clear from the beginning she wasn't interested in that kind of commitment until much further down the road.

For the first time in my life, I was willing to make long-term plans with a woman, as long as she didn't want children.

The one thing I was certain of was that I never wanted to be like my father. And the only way to guarantee that was never to become one.

CHAPTER 20

"No, I can't do it!" I insisted, gripping the skillet handle with both hands.

"You can do this. Don't worry, I'm going to help you." Jack came up behind me and put his strong hands over mine, helping me hold it. He nibbled my earlobe, sending thrills running through me. I couldn't help but giggle.

"This is serious," I chastised playfully. "I need to concentrate or I'll never be able to do it right."

"Flipping an omelet is easy," Jack soothed.

"Yeah, because what goes up must come down, probably all over the floor," I said nervously.

"That's not true," Jack nuzzled my neck.

"You can't deny gravity," I insisted.

"You can do this. You just need to have confidence in your ability to do it. I believe in you," Jack encouraged, and I already felt better.

"Okay, on the count of three," I said. Jack helped me move the pan in just the right way to slide the omelet loosely on the nonstick skillet. We counted down together, and then I tossed the concoction of eggs, ham, and cheese into the air, flipping it over perfectly.

"I did it!" I cried out victoriously, as I turned to face Jack. I wrapped my arms around his neck and kissed him joyously.

Suddenly, Jack lifted me into the air, and I squealed with delight as he spun me in a circle right in the middle of his kitchen.

"I knew you could do it!" he said.

As he set me back gently on the floor, "Sweet Home Alabama" came on his iPod, and he cranked up the volume. He looked at me with twinkling eyes and said, "This deserves a celebration. Let's dance."

Before I could even respond, he grabbed me by the hands and was twirling me around the kitchen. We danced to the beat, bumping hips. His goofy dance moves made me laugh.

There was no denying I had fallen for him. Every time he gazed into my eyes with his incredible deep blue ones, my heart absolutely melted, and the feelings I had for him only grew stronger every time he smiled or we had sex or he made me laugh.

Yes, I had fallen for the man I once thought was an obnoxious boss from hell, and I had fallen hard.

Suddenly, I noticed a strange smell in the air and cried out, "The eggs! Crap! I hope breakfast isn't ruined."

"It's impossible for you to ruin anything," Jack insisted. "Besides, there's nothing better than the taste of burnt cheese."

He set the plates of food on the sunny breakfast table of his lavish house and pulled out my chair for me. I took the first bite, and despite my doubts, I had to admit the omelet he'd taught me to make tasted amazing.

Jack grinned at me sexily and said, "See, I knew you could be a good cook."

"That's only because I had a great teacher." I smiled back at him flirtatiously.

Jack really was a terrific teacher when he wanted to be, with his patience and communication skills. It was too bad he never wanted to have kids, because it was obvious he would make an amazing father. He just didn't know it yet.

I empathized with him about the abuse he'd suffered as a child, but I had a feeling being a parent would bring him the unconditional love and happiness he so richly deserved.

If only he knew that too.

Jack had such a huge heart. I still couldn't believe he was giving me a bonus to help pay off my debts. I was determined not only to earn every penny of it through hard work at Lion, but also to donate to his charities as soon as I was able. Maybe it would even be with the profits from my jewelry company some day in the future.

Maddie was working on building the website for me on her days off. I'd come up with the name Made With Love Jewelry, since it embodied how I felt when I was creating the pieces. Maddie was just as certain as Jack was that I could build a successful business. But I'd never abandon Lion now that I had fallen for Jack. So my little hobby would probably always remain just that.

As we were wrapping up breakfast, a call came in on Jack's cell phone from Grayson, and he took it into his home office to talk while I cleaned up the dishes and loaded them into the dishwasher. When he came back into the kitchen, Jack was flushed with chagrin.

"Well, the cat's out of bag," he said with a shrug.

"What do you mean?" Instantly, my heart began to race.

Please God, don't let him say what I think he's about to say.

"Apparently the whole office knows you and I are sleeping together."

"Oh, no!" I began, but he held his hand up.

"But Grayson says we can both relax. Apparently, no one gives a shit as long as our jobs are getting done."

"Really?" I asked, unbelieving.

"Really."

As his words sank in, I felt a huge weight lifted from my shoulders.

I laughed at the irony and said, "So all that effort we put into keeping it a secret was just a waste?"

"Don't worry. Apparently, we weren't that good at it anyway," Jack teased before kissing me sensuously.

We rode to work together in his car. I fought off sleep as I sat in the passenger's seat. I figured I was drowsy because Jack had been keeping me up at night. Or we'd been keeping each other up, to be exact. Tonight, I'd have to get better rest.

As we approached the office, though, I worried that everyone would treat me differently now that they all knew I was sleeping with the boss, but no one did. It was a huge relief to no longer have to hide the truth.

"Does this mean we can openly hold hands now when we go out to dinner?" I asked Jack with a playful smile.

"It does, but I won't be dining with you tonight," Jack said apologetically. "There's some kind of a glitch with our security system at one of the Hotel Vista locations. Grayson and I are going to meet with Howard Morris about it. Hopefully, it's an easy fix."

"Okay, let's have dinner tomorrow instead," I said, already missing him.

"Deal," Jack agreed as he gave me a quick kiss goodbye.

No sooner had Jack and Grayson left in the elevator than Maddie popped up behind me. Her brightly colored hair and matching glasses never ceased to amuse me. Today, they were both a wonderful shade of purple.

"You can hold hands with me during dinner tonight," she said cheekily.

"As long as you don't tell me any of your terrible jokes or puns," I teased.

She held up her hand in a solemn vow.

It had been too long since we'd had a girls' night together, so we decided to go to our favorite deli when we got off work that evening.

As the waitress served our food, Maddie asked her, "Hey, how many computer programmers does it take to screw in a light bulb? None! That's an issue with hardware, not programming!"

The waitress didn't laugh, but I did. Mostly because Maddie was cracking up so hard at her own terrible joke.

She winked at me and said, "You never said I couldn't tell the jokes to other people."

"You got me there," I agreed. It felt good to relax and be silly with a friend. I mused how much I loved my life here in LA. Everything was so perfect, and I never wanted it to change.

When we finished eating, Maddie pulled out her laptop and showed me the progress she'd been making with the website for Made With Love Jewelry.

It was exciting and scary to realize my dream of having my own business could become a reality. Only I wasn't sure if I could ever really go through with it. My life was going so good right now. Was it really worth risking everything to follow some pipe dream? What if no one bought my jewelry? What if I failed?

"Am I boring you with too much technobabble?" Maddie asked as I yawned. I was staring at her computer screen, trying to concentrate, but I needed a nap.

"I'm sorry. I just don't have any energy today," I apologized, unable to figure out why I'd been so tired lately. "Maybe I should go home and get to bed early."

We hugged goodbye and I went home and crashed into bed even though the night was still early.

I must have gotten some food poisoning from the deli, because the next morning, I was extremely sick. Even just thinking about food made me want to vomit.

"I can't come in to work yet," I said to Jack when I called in sick. "I'll see if I can drag myself in later. But I know I'll need to recover tonight. Give me a rain check for dinner?"

"Of course. Just concentrate on getting better. I'm lost here without you," Jack said. His words made me smile.

I managed to show up to work by the early afternoon when I was feeling a bit more like myself, but I was surprised to see Maddie was feeling perfectly fine.

"Why aren't you sick?" I asked her. "We both had the same thing last night."

"Beats me." Maddie shrugged as she pushed her glasses back up her nose.

The next day, I woke up feeling sick again.

"I'm sorry to miss more work. And I have to cancel our dinner plans again," I said to Jack, feeling terrible about canceling twice.

"It's all right. The important thing is for you to take care of yourself," Jack said.

By the afternoon, I was able to make my way to the office, though I felt too exhausted to have dinner with Jack. I went home from work and fell asleep early.

After the third day of this pattern, I was panicking.

This clearly wasn't food poisoning.

On Thursday morning, I looked at my calendar and counted days on my fingers. My eyes went wide as I realized my period was late. Very late. I supposed I'd been so busy with Jack and work that I hadn't noticed.

Uh-oh.

I needed a pregnancy test. Immediately. But I didn't have

time to get one before work, and lunch was cut short by one emergency after another. My thoughts swirled around me as I considered whether I could be pregnant. I struggled to focus on my tasks in the office. I wanted desperately to get to the drugstore all day. But I couldn't find the time to slip away to buy a test.

The worry and tension built up inside me as my mind grew more distracted. I found myself avoiding Jack so he wouldn't see me like this. I knew I wasn't acting like my usual content and optimistic self. Today, I was a nervous wreck. I didn't want him to think there was anything wrong between us, so it was best to keep a little distance. So much was going on at work anyway, and I didn't think he noticed.

After work, I rushed to the drugstore and hurried back home in a frenzy.

"So, how long do we have to wait?" Stuart held my hand as we sat on the edge of my bed, staring across the room at the tiny plastic test resting on my bathroom counter.

"The instructions said we'll have results in five minutes." My palm was sweating as I clutched Stuart's hand tighter.

"Do you really think you're pregnant?" Stuart asked, sounding even more nervous than I was, which was impossible. My heart was pounding so fast, I could feel my pulse as it rushed through my body.

"I don't know, but my period is twelve days late, and I've always been regular," I said, wishing he'd talk about anything else.

I was freaking out on the inside, and I just needed to know for sure that I was panicking for nothing. A negative test result would go a long way towards making me feel better. There were a lot of reasons my period could be late. It wasn't unreasonable to hope the test could be negative.

Suddenly, the timer I'd set on my phone went off, and I walked slowly toward the stick. My heart was in my throat, and it was impossible to swallow. My hands trembled as I picked up the pregnancy test. I could barely read the results, my hands were shaking so badly.

"Well? What does it say?" Stuart was dying to know.

Instead of answering, I crumpled into a heap on the floor and sobbed despondently.

"What am I going to do?"

Stuart held me and rocked me, trying to comfort me, but I was distraught. My life was crumbling around me.

I just couldn't figure out how this could have happened to me. Jack and I were always careful, using a condom every time. Neither one of us wanted children at this stage in our lives. At least, I wanted them much later.

And in Jack's case, he'd made it clear he *never* wanted kids. Now, his words haunted me.

Being pregnant before I was ready was a devastating blow. It was all so overwhelming. The idea of raising a child right now seemed impossible.

Eventually, I cried out all my tears. I washed my face in the sink and then collapsed in my bed. Stuart met me in my room and handed me a tall glass of ice water.

"What are you going to do?" he asked.

I sighed. "I guess I'm going to become a mother."

My own words sent a shock through my system. Me, a mother? Already? I thought I'd have a few more years before I became a mom. And I never planned on being a single mother either.

Stuart nodded. "Normally, I'd make margaritas, but I guess that's out for at least nine months." I smiled wanly. He gripped my hand and said, "You know, you can count on me to be there for you through this whole thing."

"I know, Stuart. Thank you for being such a wonderful friend." I smiled gratefully.

It was kind of him to offer to help, but I knew it wouldn't

be enough. A baby needed stability, not a life in the bachelor pad of a real estate agent with a revolving door of boyfriends coming through all the time. And not with a mother who only had a relatively new career. No matter how good my job was at Lion, it was entry level. I'd wanted to reach a higher level in my career before a baby came long.

And most of all, I wanted the baby to have a father.

I'd dreamed all my life of becoming a mother. But in those dreams, I'd always been married with a stable life and a permanent home.

Sipping my water, I said wistfully, "I wonder what Jack will say about all this."

"You're not going to tell him yet, are you?" Stuart gasped loudly.

"He *is* the father," I pointed out.

"Yeah, but there's no harm in waiting."

"Why would I wait?" I was flabbergasted. "He might want to come to doctor appointments or go with me to parenting classes."

Stuart rolled his eyes and said, "You said Jack doesn't want kids. So, when you tell him you're pregnant, what do you think will happen? He'll probably end the relationship, and then working together will become so awkward you'll probably quit your job. If I were you, I'd keep this pregnancy a secret as long as possible before bringing that mess upon yourself."

"That's ridiculous!" I said, shaking my head. "I have to tell him."

I picked up the phone. I dialed Jack's number, but as it rang, doubt began to creep up in my mind. What if Stuart was right and Jack didn't want anything to do with me or the baby?

"I'm glad you called," Jack said when he answered. "There's a big emergency with the company. Howard Morris called, and the glitch we thought we'd fixed has gotten much worse. Grayson and I have to drive to Vista Hotel first thing in the morning to see if we can solve it from there."

He sounded really stressed. I realized I couldn't tell him I was pregnant like this. Not during a work crisis, and especially not over the phone. My news would have to wait until tomorrow, after he resolved the issue with Vista.

"Is there anything I can do to help?" I offered.

"Yes, take care of the office for me while we're gone. If anyone is up to the task, it's you," he said, and I blushed from the praise. "That is, if you're feeling better?"

"Don't worry, I can do it," I assured him. Then more hesitantly, "When you get back, we need to spend some time alone together. There's something I want to tell you."

"Sure, we can do that. But now I've got to focus on solving this crisis," Jack said.

We hung up, and I saw Stuart staring right at me with a knowing look on his face.

"You made the right choice, sweetie," Stuart said. "Avoid telling him for as long as you can."

"I'm not going to keep this pregnancy a secret," I said, recoiling. "No matter what happens with our relationship, romantically or at work, it doesn't matter. Jack is still this baby's father, and he deserves to know about it as soon as possible."

"At least you'll be entitled to some major child support," Stuart quipped.

"I'm not after his money. I'm telling Jack because every child deserves a father. Jack might just surprise you by wanting to have a real relationship with our baby. If he chooses not to be involved, that's on him, but I want to know in my heart that I gave him the opportunity."

"I think you're making a big mistake." Stuart threw up his hands in exasperation.

"No, the mistake would be trying to keep something this big a secret. I'm telling him the moment he gets back, and that's final."

I went to bed firm in my convictions, but I tossed and turned all through the night, hoping that once Jack knew about the baby, he would want to be a father. And worrying about how I would manage if he didn't want to be one.

In my heart, I already felt like a mother. I just hoped I wouldn't have to be one all alone.

CHAPTER 21

"Whoa! Take the curves a little slower!" Grayson shouted out as he gripped the dashboard with fear. "We want to get to Vista Hotel in one piece."

"I'm sorry, buddy." I glanced down at the speedometer and was startled by just how fast I was going. I took my foot off the gas immediately and let the car slow to a safer speed, thankful there weren't any traffic cops around.

"Your mind is a million miles away," Grayson observed. "Don't sweat this glitch thing. We've had worse problems before and we've managed to fix them. We've come a long way since we were just a couple of broke kids in a garage with nothing but an idea and ambition."

"I know. It's not that," I said coolly, although I'd have been lying if I'd said the Vista Hotel account wasn't extremely important and weighing heavily on my mind. However, I had a much bigger concern that I couldn't stop obsessing about.

"What is it then?" Grayson asked. He put his feet up on my dash and said casually, "You might as well tell me, because you know I'll figure it out sooner or later. Nobody knows you better than me, old friend."

It was true. Before Violet, the only person I ever confided in about my parents was Grayson. He was there for me during those dark days when I didn't have anyone and it bonded us like brothers.

Heaving a heavy breath, I said, "It's my relationship with Violet."

"Ha! Bullshit!" Grayson blasted. "I've never seen you happier with a woman in your entire life. She's the perfect match for you, and you know it."

"I thought so, but I'm beginning to think she doesn't feel the same way," I confessed.

"What are you talking about?" Grayson put his feet down and really listened with concern. I told him about how strange and standoffish she'd been acting all week, avoiding me and canceling dates.

"She hasn't slept over at my place once all week. And when I try to be close to her at work when no one's looking, she avoids me. I don't understand what's going on. Violet used to be so affectionate. We couldn't keep our hands off each other."

"Maybe she's one of those women who just gets a thrill out of having a taboo relationship," Grayson suggested. "When things were a secret, she was all over you, but now that the whole office knows, it's not nearly as thrilling."

"No, that couldn't be it." I furrowed my brow as I gripped the steering wheel tighter. "Violet's a terrible liar. She never liked having to keep our relationship secret and was genuinely delighted when I told her we didn't have to anymore. Something else is definitely bothering her."

"Do you think it's another guy?" Grayson suggested with hesitation.

"No. She's not like that. She's way too honest and caring. I don't think she would ever cheat on me. She'd end things first."

With a heavy sigh, I realized I knew just what was going on. "Violet must have gotten tired of our relationship. We always said from the beginning that it was no strings attached. Either one of us could end it at any time. She must have sensed that I was developing feelings for her, and since she doesn't reciprocate, she must want to call things off."

"Do you really think that's what's going on?" Grayson sounded unconvinced. "I've seen the way she looks at you. I've got to believe she feels for you the same way you do for her."

I shook my head vehemently. "No, she was very adamant, she didn't want anything serious between us. She wanted to keep things casual so it didn't interfere with her independence. I've driven her away by getting too close." I heaved a sigh. "She said she wants to talk to me privately when we get back. She plans to end our relationship, I know it. It's over between us."

"So, that's an easy fix," Grayson shrugged. "Just tell her you want to keep things casual."

"Even if I'm ready to be committed to her?" I asked.

Grayson shrugged and said, "You won't get the chance to be committed to her if she ends things."

"I don't want to lose her. I guess I'd rather have a casual relationship with her than none at all."

"So, tell her," Grayson said as we pulled into the parking lot of Vista Hotel.

As we strode into the building, I forced myself to focus on the task at hand. There was no time to dwell on my relationship with Violet any longer.

But as we met with Howard, a dark cloud hovered over me. A fear tugged at the back of my mind – an ominous worry that things were about to change with Violet forever.

CHAPTER 22

VIOLET

"We're on our way back." Jack's voice came through the phone as he drove back to the office.

"Did you fix the glitch?" I asked anxiously, hoping he had so I could finally tell him my big news.

"Not yet, but I'm working on it," Jack said. There was a long, awkward pause. Then he said, "You know, I want to say that I'm glad our relationship is no strings attached. It's nice to be able to keep things casual without trying to get serious."

My heart sank through my chest. So, Jack still didn't want any commitments. Not with me, and much less with a family. The announcement hurt, and tears stung my eyes.

"Do you really think so?" I asked.

"Yes, I do. You don't have to worry about me wanting to change our relationship. We can keep things just the way they are indefinitely. I'll see you soon," Jack said.

Then, he was gone.

I sat there at my desk holding the phone and trying not to cry.

He didn't care for me as much as I cared for him. My

heart constricted as the weight of Jack's words settled in my chest.

Maybe Stuart was right and it was a mistake to tell Jack about the pregnancy. But I'd promised myself I would tell him today.

For the rest of the morning, I couldn't stop thinking about what Jack had said. He didn't want strings attached. How would he react when he found out I was carrying his child? Maybe I'd lose him forever. Would he even want to be involved in the child's life? Would my baby grow up never knowing his father?

Worrying so much only made me feel nauseous, or maybe it was the pregnancy. My morning sickness had been getting worse and sometimes lasted all day.

For lunch, I tried to nibble on a cracker at my desk, hoping it would settle my stomach. But after just a few bites, I ended up having to rush to the ladies' room.

When I returned from the restroom, I heard a commotion at the reception desk. A blonde woman I'd never seen before was giving Kate a hard time.

"Don't tell me he's not here! I need to speak to Jack McCann now, and I'm not leaving until I do," she stated aggressively. Her platinum hair was piled high on her head in thick curls, and her long nails were the same shade of blue as the tacky dress she was wearing. She teetered over to Kate in her five-inch heels, trying to bully her, and I decided to step in and rescue the shy receptionist.

"I'm sorry, Jack McCann is not available at the moment. I'm his executive assistant. Perhaps I can help you."

The blonde looked me up and down appraisingly and then sneered.

"No. This is a private matter between me and Jack. I'm sure he's told all his little employees to cover for him, but you can let him know he can't ignore me forever. I'll be standing right here waiting for him until he talks to me."

Her entire demeanor, from her bunched shoulders to the way she placed her hands on her hips, was like an alley cat ready to scratch someone's eyes out, but I refused to be intimidated.

"You're welcome to wait in the lobby, but I assure you Mr. McCann is out of the building," I said evenly. "Perhaps you'd like to leave a message."

The angry blonde paced the floor for a few minutes, obviously considering what to do. I returned to my desk, pretending to concentrate on my work, but I kept one eye on her the entire time. There was something familiar about her, and the vibe she was giving off was definitely hostile. Part of me was wondering if I should call building security to escort her out, but I hated to cause a scene if I didn't have to. Maybe she'd just get bored and leave.

Finally, my wish came true. The blonde reached into her purse and thrust an envelope toward me so brusquely, it nearly slapped me in the face.

"Here, deliver this letter to Jack. It explains everything."

"I will," I assured her, but she just rolled her eyes at me as if she were entrusting a valuable treasure to a complete imbecile. Just to irk her, I asked, "And who shall I say it's from?"

"Tell him Ashley Stokes sends her regards." She then turned her back on me and strode out of the office with her chin in the air and her ass swaying.

For a moment, I stared at the envelope, debating what to do with it. I decided not to open it. After all, Ashley had said it was a personal matter between her and Jack.

Then, I remembered he had instructed me to take care of the office while he was gone. Maybe it was something that would need immediate attention.

Besides, the curiosity was killing me.

I tore into the envelope and found a single piece of paper inside. The envelope fell to the floor as I read the hand-written letter, giddy with anticipation as to what it could possibly say.

That feeling of elation quickly turned into one of disgust, and my stomach roiled with horror at what she had written.

It was an extortion letter. Ashley Stokes was demanding Jack pay off all her debts or else she would make up a string of lies to ruin his career. She even threatened to tell the media Jack was using the cameras of his security system to spy on his female clients when they were in the shower or getting dressed in the privacy of their own homes.

I gasped as I stared at the paper.

It was an outrageous and horrible lie, but the public might believe it. If they did, she would ruin Jack's reputation and his business would be destroyed. Every employee at Lion would be out of a job, including myself. Worst of all, the man I cared deeply for — and the father of my child — would have his entire life ruined.

She ended the letter with:

You might think you're too good for me. But just remember, what goes up must come down.

There was no signature, just the ugly promise of her threats.

I couldn't let her get away with doing this to Jack.

I fought off the panic threatening to overwhelm me. I had to keep my wits about me. I needed to contact Jack and tell him about this letter so he could take it to the police right away, but he was driving at the moment. Chewing my lip, I debated what to do.

Suddenly, the elevator doors opened and Jack came striding out. My elation was cut short however, when

Grayson and Howard Morris came walking out right behind him.

"Hi, Violet. Please don't forward any calls to my office for the rest of the afternoon. We'll be in a private meeting," Jack instructed as he led them into his office.

I acknowledged him with a smile, but the panic must have shown in my eyes, because Jack paused and stared at me.

"Is everything all right?" he asked in a low voice.

I wanted to tell him about the letter so badly, but Grayson and Howard were both standing right there along with him, staring at me. I couldn't let anyone else know about the extortion letter, most especially the company's prized client.

My pulse rushed in my ears, and I felt myself panicking. Suddenly, I realized I was still holding the vile letter in my hands, and I quickly shoved it into the top drawer of my desk.

"Everything is fine," I stammered. Jack seemed satisfied with the lie, even though I'd done a terrible acting job. He entered his office with Grayson and Howard and closed the door, leaving me alone with the extortion letter hidden in my desk and no idea what to do about it.

Jack needed to know about this letter as soon as possible, but he also needed to know about the pregnancy. Telling him either would be devastating for him, but not telling him would only make things worse.

Holding my belly with one hand and locking the drawer shut with the other, I was completely torn about what to do.

I hated keeping secrets, and now I had two really big ones.

CHAPTER 23

JACK

"I'll give you till tomorrow to fix this glitch, or I'm canceling my account with you," Howard Morris said, and stormed out of my office.

I couldn't say I could fault him for blaming me. In fact, if anyone was to blame, it was me. I was the one in charge of the programmers at Lion.

I had Violet gather them all together. She kept looking at me with big, scared eyes like there was something she needed to tell me.

But as worried as I was about what she needed to tell me, I didn't have time for that now. The failure in the Vista system was urgent, and all of our jobs were at stake. Since getting the Vista Hotels account, we'd made expensive upgrades to our systems and staff. If we lost Vista now, we'd be screwed.

I worked side by side with the programmers for hours, trying to find the bug in the code to fix the glitch. My team was the best, and I knew if anyone could do it, it was them.

They worked for hours well into the night before Maddie finally cried out with victory.

"I think I got it!"

It was like finding the golden ticket in a Wonka Bar. Grayson and I rushed to her desk to see for ourselves.

We tested her repair and determined that she had indeed solved the glitch in the system. When I called Howard Morris, he was satisfied and agreed to keep his account with us.

I made the announcement to the room, and the whole office erupted into cheers.

"Maddie, you are a true hero!" I held up her arm like a boxing champion.

It was a sign of how exhausted she was that she didn't even gloat. "Thanks," she simply said, pushing her colorful glasses back up the bridge of her nose.

Then, I looked out at the room of hardworking employees and said, "Drinks at the bar are on me!"

They cheered again and filed out the door, ready for a well-earned celebration at the neighborhood bar. They'd all worked hard and deserved to let off some steam.

As the office emptied, I realized Violet wasn't among the crowd. I knew she had hung around while the programmers worked. I'd told her to go home, but she'd insisted on staying. Now, she was nowhere to be found. I searched the office.

"Aren't you coming, Jack?" Maddie asked as she spotted me while she waited for the elevator.

I waved her off. "I'll catch up with you guys later."

Maddie nodded and got on the elevator.

Finally, I found Violet near her desk. She sat in a chair behind the filing cabinets. It almost looked like she was hiding.

"There you are. I feel like we've hardly seen each other all week." I held my arms out to her, but she avoided my embrace.

"I know. It's been a difficult week," she said, her eyes cast down.

I'd hoped what I'd said to her earlier on the phone would have pleased her, but maybe we just needed some time alone together. I gave her my most charming grin. "Thank goodness the week's over. What do you say we run away to the beach house for the weekend? We could relax and spend some quality time together."

"That sounds wonderful, but there's something we need to talk about first," she said, looking strangely pale and nervous. Clearly my attempts to placate her had failed.

My heart became a heavy lump in my throat, making it hard to breathe. This was it. She was going to tell me she was ending our relationship.

I looked around to make sure we were all alone in the office. No point delaying the inevitable. I braced myself for what was coming, and said gently, "I'm listening."

Violet couldn't even look me in the eye. She drew in a heavy breath. I expected her drop the hammer, but she surprised me. "Do you know a woman named Ashley Stokes?"

"Who?" I was completely thrown by the question.

The name sounded familiar, but it had been such a shitty day, my mind was fried. I couldn't remember who she was.

"You must know her. Blonde, pretty, with dyed platinum hair and a terrible sense of fashion," Violet replied.

Suddenly her face came rushing back to me. Ashley was that woman Grayson tried to set me up with months ago at the bar, but she wasn't my type, and I'd sent her home in a cab. For a while, she'd tried relentlessly to get me to go on a date with her, so I blocked her number and eventually forgot all about her. Violet must have found some of her old messages and thought I was cheating on her with Ashley.

No wonder Violet had been acting so strangely. What a relief! A weight lifted off my shoulders.

"She's nobody to me," I explained. "Ashley is some woman Grayson tried to set me up with long ago. Before you came into the picture."

I pulled her into my arms, hoping the misunderstanding was now resolved, but Violet pushed me away and said, "You have a big problem now because of her."

I never would have expected Violet to be the jealous type. I needed to soothe her fears right away, so I said gently, "I never went on a single date with Ashley. You're the only woman I want to have a relationship with."

I expected my words would make Violet feel better. Instead, she looked even paler than before. Handing me the key to her desk, her voice had an odd tremor as she said, "Just look in the top drawer of my desk."

"Okay." I walked over to the desk and unlocked the top drawer, having no fucking clue what I might find in there. It was full of all sorts of miscellaneous junk, notepads, pencils, and rubber bands.

"Read the folded-up paper," Violet instructed.

I found it easily, a piece of plain white paper with hand-writing on it in blue ink. I felt excited and curious as I began to read. Had Violet written me a dirty letter – or a profession of her feelings for me?

It only took me a few sentences into the letter to realize it was something very fucking different. I stopped and read it over from the beginning, the anger and horror building up inside me.

The letter demanded that I pay off all Violet's debts or she would ruin my career by spreading vicious lies.

She didn't sign it but ended it with the words *what goes up must come down*. It was a phrase Violet used often, so I knew it was her.

My gut clenched.

Consumed by the pain of her betrayal, I crumpled the extortion letting into my fist and stared at Violet.

"How could you do something like this to me?" I growled with bristling rage, barely able to control my hostility. "Is this some act of revenge because you thought I was cheating on you with Ashley? Or was it your plan from the beginning to use me for my money?"

"What? No! The letter isn't from me!"

Violet tried to deny it, but I didn't believe her. I quickly realized she really could lie after all.

My heart was breaking. I'd never felt so betrayed or violated in all my life. Being taken advantage of by the other women who'd been after my money had hurt, but not like this. I'd foolishly believed Violet was different. I'd opened my heart to her and told her things I'd never told anyone. I'd felt a real connection with her, and now I realized it was just her way of tricking me so she could take advantage of me too. I should have known she was too good to be true. No one could really be that perfect. No woman could truly care for me the way I thought Violet did.

Trembling with anger, I threw the letter to the floor and snarled, "It was in your locked desk drawer. You gave me the key. You told me to read it. Who else would it be from?"

"The blonde, Ashley. It's why I asked you about her."

"Bullshit!" I snapped. "Not even Ashley would stoop this low. Besides, she and I never even went out on a date. I haven't seen her in months. I'm sure she's forgotten all about me. Why would she try to blackmail me now? It was you, Violet. Just admit it."

"I don't know why she would try to blackmail you now," Violet said, her voice strained. "But it was her."

"I can't believe you take me for a fool like this, Violet," I said. "It's in your handwriting. It's written using phrases you use."

"You've hardly even seen my handwriting," she countered. "Every communication we have in this office is electronic."

I shook my head. She was trying to dupe me, but I recognized the truth when I saw it.

"How could you do this, Violet? I knew you were worried about your debt, but to try to extort me? And what I don't understand is why you're denying it now. Are you too ashamed to admit it to my face? Is this some kind of a sick game to you?"

"It's not a game, and I'm not lying to you." Violet pinched the bridge of her nose.

To my disgust, she kept refusing to admit that she had written the letter and was after my money. I pushed her to tell the truth, hoping that maybe I could forgive her if she would only apologize and take responsibility for her actions. After all, I had developed strong feelings for her, and I hated to lose what we had together. But if she couldn't even be honest with me about writing the letter, there was no hope for us.

The more she denied it, the more hurt and angry I became.

"Stop giving me these outrageous lies!" I finally shouted in frustration.

"You know what?" Violet was pale and trembling. "If you can't trust me and believe what I said, then – then I guess I can't be with you anymore."

She looked so vulnerable and hurt, I wanted to pull her into my arms and comfort her. I had to remind myself that it was just an act to manipulate me, just like she'd been doing all along. Forcing myself to put up a tough front, I crossed my arms over my chest.

"Fine," I said. "There was no way I was going to keep

having a relationship with you after you tried to extort money from me anyway."

"I'm not just talking about our relationship," Violet cried. "I'm talking about being your executive assistant too. I never want to look at you again, Jack. I quit!"

I watched in stunned silence as she stormed out the door. I could hear my heart breaking with every clack of her heels on the floor.

As the elevator doors shut behind her, I knew my life would never be the same without her.

CHAPTER 24

VIOLET

"*H*ey, sweetie. I made you some tea."

Stuart entered my bedroom gingerly, carrying a steaming mug of chamomile and a plate of blueberry scones.

"Thanks, Stuart, but I just want to be alone." I rolled over in my bed and pulled the covers over my head.

"You've got to rehydrate, sweetie, or you'll ruin your skin," Stuart chastised. "I know you were up crying all night long. I gave you privacy to mourn your relationship over the weekend, but today starts a brand-new week. What do you say we go downtown and have a makeover day?"

"I don't feel like going anywhere," I groaned, but Stuart wouldn't let up.

He pulled the covers off of me and forced me to sit up in bed. With his hands on his hips, he said, "I know morning sickness is a bitch, but you really should try to eat or drink something. If you don't like scones, I'll make you anything else you want for breakfast. You name it."

I really didn't want anything, but I knew from experience,

the best way to get rid of Stuart was to appease him, so I dipped the scone in the tea, and took a small bite.

"Happy now?" I asked with a sarcastic grin that bordered on psychotic.

"Not as happy as I'd be if you'd never started going out with Jack McCann in the first place," Stuart bemoaned. "It's all my fault. I was the one who introduced you to that asshole. I just knew he was my richest client and that he needed an assistant. I had no idea he intended to take advantage of you and then break your heart."

"It wasn't like that." I suddenly felt the need to defend him for some reason. "We had a mutual agreement to sleep with each other, no strings attached. It's not like he broke my heart. I was just up crying all night because I lost my job, that's all."

"Then why can't you say his name?" Stuart asked, calling me out on my obvious lie.

"I *can* say his name," I said, doubling down on my denial.

"Then let me hear you say it." Stuart wouldn't let up.

"Fine, it's Jack. Jack McCann," I snapped, but the moment I said his name, my stomach roiled uncontrollably. I sprang from bed, ran into the bathroom, and vomited in the toilet.

Stuart was by my side in a flash, holding my hair and crooning words of sympathy. "I know he broke your heart, sweetie, but screw him. There are plenty of other men out there far more worthy of your affection."

"Yeah, right!" I broke down and cried with all the pain of my broken heart. "Jack started out as a jerk, but the more I got to know the real him inside, we formed a special connection. He was kind, caring, generous, and the sex was the best I've ever had. We were so happy together. I thought we had something special, but you should have seen the way he looked at me when he accused me of writing that extortion letter. He hates me. He's convinced I'm a liar and a gold digger. I'll never be able to convince him the feelings I have for him are real, and I'm never going to feel this way for anyone else."

I sobbed for all the pain of my crushed heart. I'd never felt so miserable or broken-hearted. Stuart held me and said, "It's going to be okay, Vi. I promise. If you need anything, just tell me, and I'll be there for you."

"Thanks." I smiled up at my best friend, grateful to have him in my life. "There *is* something…"

I hesitated to finish the thought, but Stuart leaned in with anticipation. "What is it, Violet?"

"It's just that I still haven't told Jack about the baby."

"You can't seriously still be planning to tell him now that you've seen his true colors!" Stuart was aghast.

"I don't expect it to change the problems between us, but he is still the baby's father. Even if Jack and I never reconcile, my baby still deserves to have two caring parents."

"And you think that cold-hearted brute qualifies?" Stuart scoffed.

"Jack has a real tender side. I've seen him be incredibly sweet and generous. I know that if he could just lower the walls around his heart, he'd make an amazing father."

"If you say so," Stuart said, unbelieving.

"For the sake of my baby, I want to give Jack that chance. If I have to raise this baby alone, I'm prepared to do that, but one day, my child might ask about its father, and I want to be able to honestly say that I wasn't the one who kept them apart."

"Okay, fine. For the baby, I'll do it." Stuart acquiesced, and I wanted to hug him. He rolled his eyes. "What do you need? Do you want me to drive you to his office? Go in with you to talk to him? Anything."

"Nothing like that. I just need to borrow your phone. He's refusing to take my calls."

"Do you really think you should tell him over the phone?" Stuart scrunched his face as he handed me his cell.

"No, I'm going to tell him in person, but I don't think I should drop by unannounced. Even after everything that happened between us, he should still agree to a civilized meeting."

"Okay, I'll give you some privacy." Stuart handed me his phone and closed my bedroom door with a sympathetic smile.

I felt cool and confident as I dialed Jack's number. I could do this. I could call my ex with detached professionalism. This wasn't about us or our relationship. I was doing this for the sake of my child, not to cry and beg him to take me back.

I was totally in control of my emotions as the phone rang, until suddenly Jack's voice came on the line.

"Jack McCann," he answered.

My heart froze in my chest, and it was difficult to speak.

I knew in that moment I would never be over Jack. I would always care for him with all my heart. Telling him about our baby meant offering him a chance to be involved in my life, not just our baby's. That involvement in my life could last for the next eighteen years – if not forever. I'd be cursed with always seeing him and never being able to call him mine. It was a heartbreaking sentence to endure, but for the sake of my child, I would do it.

"Hello, Jack. It's me," I said bravely. "We need to meet."

CHAPTER 25

JACK

"Knock, knock. Hey, buddy, do you have a minute?" Grayson stuck his head in my office door to find me sitting at my desk with my head in my hands.

"Not now," I growled, hoping he'd leave, but Grayson knew me too well for that. Ignoring my words, he strolled into my office and put his feet up on my desk.

"What happened to you this weekend?" he asked. "You promised to buy everyone drinks at the bar then never showed. I had to cover the tab. You're welcome, by the way. Then I tried getting a hold of you all weekend, and my calls keep going to voicemail. What happened? You and Violet must have had one hell of a time!"

"You could say that," I said tightly. I pulled the crumpled extortion letter out of my pocket and handed it to him. I watched his face as he read it, thinking the words silently in my mind as his eyes moved across the paper. I'd read it so many times over the weekend, I'd memorized it. I didn't know why I didn't throw the fucking thing away. I should have, but I needed it to fuel my anger. Without it, all I felt was crushed and heartbroken.

"We need to turn this over to the police!" Grayson was on his feet at once.

"No, I don't want to press charges," I said. My voice was numb, like my body.

"We can't just let her get away with this." Grayson was stunned. He reached for the letter, and I gripped his arm.

"I'm not pressing charges, and that's final," I said adamantly. "She quit her job, and obviously we ended the relationship. I'm never going to see her again, and pressing charges would just be too painful."

Grayson sank down in his chair with a heavy plop. "Shit. I'm sorry, buddy. I know how much she meant to you. Is there anything I can do for you?"

"Just leave me in peace." I let my head fall onto my desk. I wanted to close my eyes and shut out the world.

Grayson opened his mouth, no doubt to tell me to charge the mountain or that there were other fish in the sea, or some similar bullshit, when my phone rang. The caller ID said it was my realtor. Normally, I would have just let it go to voicemail, but I realized this was the perfect way to get rid of Grayson. Otherwise, he'd never leave.

"I need to take this call," I said, shooing him out the door.

"Okay, I'll be in my office if you need me," Grayson said supportively. He strode from my desk with his hands shoved in his pockets, and I answered the phone.

I was shocked when I heard Violet's voice on the other end of the line, although in hindsight I should have guessed she would pull something like that. She said she wanted to meet me. My mouth went dry. Shit!

"Come to my office at twelve-thirty," I said, trying to sound cold. There was no way I was going to let her know how much my heart ached for her. "Most of the staff will be on lunch break then, and you can say what you need to say and leave."

"Thank you. There's something really important I need to tell you that needs to be said in person," Violet said. I closed my eyes, savoring the sound of her voice.

It took all my strength not to tell her how much I missed her. All I wanted to do was to apologize to her and beg her to come back to me, but why should I? She was the one who had wronged me. I had to force myself to remember that. Her feelings for me weren't real like mine were for her. She was manipulating me again, and I had to stay strong.

"I'll see you then." I hung up the phone rapidly before I could say anything I'd regret.

The hours of the morning crawled by, and I tried to keep my mind off the clock by staying busy. Seeing Violet again would be difficult. I just wished I knew what had driven her to attempt such a terrible act as extortion. Even after I'd given her a bonus to help pay her debts, it still wasn't enough for her. I wondered just how much financial trouble she could be in.

Using Lion's access to security networks, I spent the morning researching Violet's credit history and learning the true depth of her financial woes. What I discovered was devastating. Violet had spent huge amounts of money buying things for a man. Men's clothing, men's jewelry, even a fucking motorcycle.

My heart shattered into a million pieces that could never be put back together. Violet was more than just a gold digger looking for some cash.

She was a cheater too.

Our whole relationship had been one big lie right from the start. All the time I was falling for her, she secretly had a boyfriend on the side. She was just using and manipulating me with her lies all along.

Devastated, I wanted to call off my meeting with her. I couldn't bear to see her again. It was too painful. But when I looked at the clock, it was already time, and Violet was standing in my doorway.

Even though she'd broken my heart, seeing her now took my breath away. She looked amazing.

Her skin had a glow to it, and her mystical violet-gray eyes were shimmering brightly. Her full lips beckoned to be kissed, but I forced myself to resist, even though my cock ached for her.

"Here's your final paycheck. I'm sure that's what you came for," I said bitterly. I pushed the envelope across the desk toward her as she closed the door behind her and sat down across from me.

"Actually, there's something important I need to talk to you about it," she stammered.

"Is it that you have a boyfriend on the side you never told me about?" I snapped. Violet's eyes flew open wide.

"What are you talking about? I don't have a boyfriend."

"Then what are all these purchases at a motorcycle store for? I've certainly never seen you riding a motorcycle to work."

"It's not how it looks. I can explain that," Violet insisted, but I held up the report of her credit card debts in a halting gesture, silencing her.

"You can save the lies." I handed her the report confidently. I was in the right, and I had the proof to back it up. There was nothing she could say now to convince me otherwise.

"Wow. You really spied on me, didn't you?" Violet blinked, clearly shocked to have been caught red-handed. "How could you invade my privacy like this?"

"Don't act offended," I scoffed, enjoying my moment of bittersweet victory after she'd hurt me so badly. "So these are the debts you wanted me to pay? Well, you can forget it. You won't get a dime out of me."

Violet gasped, looking shocked. "This is all a misunderstanding, Jack. Don't you want to at least hear what I have to say?" She blinked back tears.

More manipulation. I wasn't going to fall for it this time.

"No, I don't want to hear any more of your bullshit. I trusted you, Violet," I said, my voice faltering for a bit then growing stronger. "I thought you were different from all those other women. I can't believe you're just like them… a gold digger. And as for your threat of spreading lies about me and my company, go ahead and try. I've got your letter as proof that you were only out for my money. Don't contact me again. I'm done being hurt by you."

Her eyes narrowed, and she stared at me for several long moments. "How – how could you think that about me? How could you do this to me, Jack?" she whispered.

"I've been wondering the same thing about you," I said, looking away. It hurt like a knife in the chest to see her suffering like that. But her pain wasn't real. It was just an act. I had to stay strong and not fall for her tricks. "Now, if you'll just sign these termination papers, I believe that concludes any business you and I may have."

Her mouth hung open for a moment and then she snapped it shut with a tight jaw and reached for the papers.

"That suits me just fine!" Violet's eyes shot sparks of lightning. She signed the papers, dropped the pen on the desk, and rose to her feet.

Then she walked out of my office and out of my life. Forever.

It should have been a relief, but it wasn't. In fact, the lump in my throat grew so large I could hardly breathe.

As much as she had hurt me, I knew I'd miss Violet Williams for the rest of my days.

CHAPTER 26

VIOLET

I held in my tears for as long as I could, determined not to let that heartless son-of-a-bitch see me cry, but the moment the elevator doors closed, I let them loose in a flood of emotion.

I cried all the way home, narrowly escaping two accidents in the process, and kept crying after I got home to the empty apartment.

I wasn't usually this emotional, but Jack had been so horribly insulting and had looked at me with such disdain. His angry words felt like daggers being thrown directly into my heart. He wouldn't even let me explain anything. He had stubbornly decided that I was a liar, and there was nothing I could do or say to change his mind.

With my throat raw and sore, I couldn't cry anymore. I dragged myself out of bed and started pacing through the apartment, my mind reeling.

After being treated like that, there was no way I was going to tell him about the baby. He probably would have accused me of lying about that too or say that the baby was just another way for me to try to get money out of him. I was going to raise this baby alone, without asking for any help from him.

I didn't want to look at him ever again, or hear his voice, or even drive past the building where he worked.

In fact, I wanted to put as much space between me and Jack McCann as I could.

I suddenly realized I was done with Los Angeles. It was time for me to go back home to Iowa.

I drank a tall glass of water to clear my throat and my mind and then picked up my cell phone. With a deep breath for courage, I dialed the number to make the most difficult call of my life.

"Hi, Mom," I said in a fake, cheery voice when she answered the line.

"Hi, Violet. I was just going to call you. Wonderful news! Guess who's having a baby?" Mom said happily.

For a moment I was speechless. How did she know? Then I realized she must have meant my sister, and my nerves calmed a bit.

Without waiting for me to respond, Mom gushed on. "Jessica is having a third child! Can you believe it? I'm so excited to see our new addition to the family."

"That's great, Mom," I said.

"Sure is," she said. "So, when are you going to settle down and get married so you can give those kids some cousins? There's nothing I'd love better than having even more grandchildren."

"Actually, Mom, that's kind of the reason I called." I decided to go ahead and say it.

"You're getting married!" Mom cried out joyously.

I knew I had to correct her before she told the whole town, booked a church, and ordered the cake.

"No, Mom. I'm not getting married, but I am having a baby."

"Wait, what?" she asked in a falling voice. It took Mom a moment to focus on what I'd said, and I remained silent. In a quiet voice, she asked, "So, you're having a baby out of *wedlock?*"

"Yes, I am," I stated simply. It pained me to disappoint her in that way, but I realized it was best just to be honest right from the start. "I'm going to raise the baby alone. The father wants nothing to do with me."

There was a long pause on the other end of the phone, and then suddenly I heard my mom call out to my father in the background, "Doug, I just got the best news!"

"Well, don't keep me in suspense, Becky. What is it?" came my dad's muffled voice.

"Violet is having a baby! I'm so happy I can't speak!"

"Well, that *is* a miracle," Dad teased, and then his booming voice came on the line. "Congratulations, Violet!"

They were the only words Dad could get in before Mom got back on the phone with him, saying joyously, "Congratulations! You're going to be a wonderful mother!"

"Thanks." I flushed, completely taken aback by just how good it felt to have my parents' approval.

"It's not under the best circumstances, but that's okay," Mom said. "You'll still be a great mother, Violet. I know it."

My heart was overflowing with happiness and relief, but there was still a heavy cloud hovering over me.

"Mom, Dad, I can't raise the baby alone here in LA. Can I come back home and live with you until I'm able to get back on my feet?"

"Of course you can," they both said in unison, making me laugh.

Mom took over the phone again, and we formed a plan together. My old bedroom was waiting for me. My parents would move out the sewing machine and boxes of junk that had accumulated in there, and Mom would put fresh linens on the bed.

"It's too bad your sister's going to be needing her bassinet, or I'm sure she would have let you borrow it." Mom blabbered on, even though I'd tried to say goodbye twice already. "That's okay, though. I'm sure we can find you something for a reasonable price. And we'll set you up with prenatal care with Jessica's doctor. She's got the best OB/GYN in town, of course."

"Mm-hmm," I mumbled in half-hearted agreement.

"Boy! It's going to be so nice having you home again. I bet Mark Hansen will think so too. I'll invite him over for supper. Who knows, maybe you two can pick up where you left off. He always said he wanted to have children one day."

I rolled my eyes in exasperation. I was about to tell her I'd rather die than marry someone as boring as Mark Hansen when, fortunately, my doorbell rang.

"Look, Mom, someone's at the door. I really have to go. I'll call you soon. Bye!" I said in a rush of words and quickly ended the phone call.

I loved my mother and was grateful for her generosity, but she could be so exhausting with her pushy, controlling nature. I was already feeling stifled by it, and I hadn't even moved back home yet.

I opened my door to see who had rescued me, and was pleasantly surprised to see Maddie standing there holding a box of all the things I'd left behind at the office.

"Maddie! What are you doing here?" I cried out happily as I let her inside.

"I brought your things." Maddie handed me the box of miscellaneous knick-knacks I'd left behind on my desk, and I set it on the table. None of it was really worth driving all the way from the office to my apartment, and she knew it.

Casting her spectacled eyes to the side, Maddie shrugged. "Plus, I really wanted to see you. I missed you."

"I missed you too." I gave her a long hug that filled a need for both of us. Finally, I let her go and asked, "How did you find me?"

"Your address was on file with the company. I put it in my computer, and it wasn't a *hard drive*," Maddie laughed that adorable giggle I'd missed so much. "Get it? Hard drive!"

I laughed aloud. I'd missed her computer geek puns, even though they were usually terrible. It felt good to joke with my friend again.

"That must have been some blowout you and Jack had when you quit," Maddie said as we sat on my couch, chatting just like we used to do at the deli. "They heard the shouting on the floor above us. Everyone in the Lion offices has been talking about it. Except no one mentions it when Jack is around, obviously. We can't do *anything* around Jack now. If you thought he was a bosshole before, you should see him now."

Hearing her talk about Jack made me painfully uncomfortable, and I fidgeted as I struggled to keep my mind from drifting away in my anxiety.

"Yeah, it's crazy," Maddie continued. "Jack is so sullen, moody, and cross. No one likes being around the guy right now. We all give him a wide berth."

I nearly jumped out of my skin at her words. In my daze, I thought she'd said the word *birth.*

My mind jumped to about a thousand conclusions at the speed of light.

"What? How did you know about the baby?" I asked, suddenly freaked out. I hadn't told anyone I was pregnant except for Stuart and my parents.

Now it was Maddie's turn to freak out. She looked at me with her mouth open.

"You're having a baby?" she asked.

We stared at each other. I finally processed what she had said, and I felt like a fool.

I hadn't wanted to tell her about the baby, but it was too late now.

And worse, I felt tears building up again. These pregnancy hormones were turning me into a blubbering mess.

I cried pitifully as I told Maddie everything about the pregnancy and how I'd planned to tell Jack he was the father – until he'd treated me like crap in his office.

Maddie listened intently as I told her my sob story.

"Want me to look at your resume, maybe perk it up a little?" she offered kindly. "I can help you find another job. Who knows, now that Jack is being such a jerk, maybe I'll even quit Lion and join you if you land at a great company."

I shook my head, moved by her offer.

"Thanks, Maddie, but I've decided to go back home to Iowa. My parents are fixing up my old bedroom. It's not my dream place, but I'll have the support of my family to help me with the baby, at least until I get back on my feet."

"What? No, you can't go!" Maddie cried, and I was touched by how hard she was taking the news. "What about your dream of being an independent woman living in the big city?"

"I tried it. Things didn't work out," I said flatly. "But my happiness doesn't matter as much anymore. I need to do what's best for my baby now."

"Well, you'll be happy to know I've finished the website for your jewelry business. You can be independent and have a career from home while still taking care of your baby."

The idea did have tremendous appeal, and a small spark of hope lit up inside me, but I quickly snuffed it out before it could turn into a flame. Making jewelry took a lot of focus. Jack had told me himself I didn't even hear him calling my name when I was doing it. What would happen if I didn't notice my baby was crying?

Besides, I doubted being a single mom would leave me much time for hobbies like making bracelets and earrings. Because that's what it really was, after all – a hobby. It was never going to pay all my bills, and I'd deluded myself to think otherwise.

"No, thank you." I shook my head sadly but adamantly. "I'm going to focus all my energy on my baby and put my foolish dreams aside."

Maddie argued with me a bit, trying to convince me it didn't have to be that way, that I didn't have to give up all my dreams. But when she saw how firmly my mind was made up, she acquiesced.

Afterwards, I walked Maddie to the door, and we said our goodbyes. We both realized it was probably the last time we would see each other, and I was surprised by just how hard it was to leave the friends I had in LA behind.

"I wish you weren't moving away," Maddie said as she hugged me. "I'm really going to miss you, Violet."

"I'm going to miss you too, but I have to do what's right for my baby, and that means going back to Iowa," I said. She nodded in understanding.

I watched as she drove away and then I closed the door for another good cry.

I got another glass of water as I sobbed. Being pregnant, I'd have to keep my fluids up if I didn't want to dehydrate to death from all the crying.

Suddenly, a firm knock came at the door, making me jump.

Had Maddie forgotten something? Or maybe it was Jack coming to apologize. I realized part of me still held hope he'd come back. I couldn't help it, even if it was silly.

Filled with curious anticipation, I opened the door. I was shocked to see two uniformed police officers standing there.

"Are you Violet Williams?" one of them asked.

Swallowing down the lump in my throat, I unconsciously put my hands protectively around my belly.

"Yes, that's me."

CHAPTER 27

JACK

I sat slumped at my desk, brooding about Violet.

How could I have been so wrong about her? I'd thought she was special. But she turned out to be just like all the rest. She was out for whatever she could get from me.

It just proved the sad and terrible fact that no woman could be trusted with my heart. It was something I'd learned when I was just a teenager, when my own mother had chosen my abuser over me.

Ever since then, every woman I'd ever trusted had deceived me so that they could use me for my money. Violet was no different. The truth hurt like hell.

A knock came at my office door. Grayson entered, looking like a dog caught in the rain.

"Can I talk to you for a minute?" he asked, and I waved him in.

"What's with you?" I asked with curiosity.

"I did something, and you're not going to like it," Grayson said, making me sit up straighter in my chair. He drew in a breath, and then just blurted it out. "I filed a police report about the extortion letter."

"I specifically told you I didn't want to press charges," I said through clenched teeth.

"I know, but you're not seeing straight. You cared about Violet too much to see the big picture. You and I have been partners from the beginning. We built up Lion out of nothing, and now we are responsible for a building full of employees. We owe it to them not to be reckless with our reputations. If someone trashes you publicly for failure to pay an extortion ransom, that hurts everybody we work for. I know you thought you were taking this risk for yourself, but as your partner and your best friend, I had to do what you couldn't."

I wanted to be mad at Grayson, but I knew he was right, at least about the risk to the company. I was filled with worry about Violet, though. As much as she'd hurt me, I didn't want her to get in trouble. Still, his eyes were pleading with me.

"Say something," he said mournfully.

"Next time promise me you'll come talk to me first instead of going behind my back."

"Next time?" Grayson couldn't help but poke fun at my misuse of phrase. "There's going to be a next time?"

"Fuck you!" I swung a fake punch at him, which he easily dodged, and we both laughed. It was the first time I'd laughed since Violet had broken my heart, and suddenly I was overcome with guilt.

Grayson must have seen it in my eyes because he slapped my back and said, "It'll be all right. These things take time."

But I didn't want to be all right over time. I knew I would miss Violet and what we had shared forever. Just because it all turned out to be a lie didn't make me miss her any less.

Suddenly, my phone rang, and I pushed my feelings down to the bottom of my gut. I cleared my throat and answered the line sounding like nothing was wrong.

"Mr. McCann, it's Officer Yorke with the LA Police

Department," the caller said. I gave Grayson a sideways glare and shooed him away.

"Yes, Officer. What can I do for you?" I asked. Grayson slipped out of my office, closing the door behind him.

"I wanted to let you know we arrested the author of the extortion letter. She signed a full confession and has pled guilty to the crime. You'll be able to press charges if you like."

Violet had so staunchly denied it to me, I was surprised she would tell the truth. But hearing she'd confessed made me feel no better, and my heart sank even lower.

"Thank you, Officer. So Violet actually confessed?"

"No. The guilty party is named Ashley Stokes," the officer stated matter-of-factly.

It was a good thing I was already sitting in my chair, or I would have fallen on my fucking ass from shock.

"Ashley? Are you sure?" I asked.

"Yes. We were able to determine right away the hand-writing on the extortion letter did not match Violet William's script. When we questioned her as to why the letter was found in her desk, she directed us to one Ashley Stokes. Ms. Stokes denied her guilt at first, but when the handwriting matched her signature, she confessed immediately and cut a deal with the district attorney, hoping for leniency from the court. Unfortunately for her, she got Judge Wendy Carson, and she does not look kindly on stunts like this."

"I can't believe it. Thank you, Officer," I said, still in shock.

The policeman gave me a few more details. Finally, we said goodbye. I hung up the phone and sat there staring at it for a long time. My throat closed in and my chest tightened like a vise.

I wandered from my office in a daze and paused in Grayson's doorway.

"I'm not feeling well. I'm going home for the day," I muttered.

"Yeah, you look like shit. You're white as a ghost." Grayson looked at me with genuine concern. "Do you need me to take you to the doctor?"

"No, I'll be all right. I just need some fresh air."

I drove slowly home, my mind struggling to process what I'd heard on the phone.

I collapsed in my bed, but I felt sick to my stomach just lying there. I needed to move, to get my blood pumping and clear my mind. I climbed on the treadmill and started running, pushing myself to my limit as punishment.

How could I have been such a stubborn fool? Violet had tried to tell me the letter was from Ashley, but I'd refused to listen. She must have hated my guts for treating her that way.

When I thought about all the things I'd said to her, the accusations and the horrible names, I hated myself more than she ever could. I just kept seeing the pain in her eyes when I yelled at her. That pitiful look of heartbreak on her beautiful face was all my fault.

I'd thought she was the one betraying me. But it turned out *I* was the monster.

I needed to apologize to her. I owed her that, even though there was no way she'd ever forgive me for falsely accusing her of trying to steal my money. Why would she? I'd treated her horribly when all she'd ever done was be good to me. I should have treated her like a princess.

Violet was the best thing that had ever happened to me. Now I'd lost her, and it was my own fucking fault!

I turned off the treadmill and let it slow to a stop. Gasping for breath, I was physically exhausted. But I still couldn't get her from my mind.

My hot, sweaty clothes were clinging to my body, strangling me. I felt claustrophobic, stifled. I stripped the shirt and shorts off in a frenzy. But I still couldn't breathe. My lungs craved fresh air.

Walking naked through the huge house, I arrived at my pool. Vast and calm, the water shimmered like a mirror. I dove into it, letting the cool water envelope my hot muscles. The temperature difference made me gasp with shock, but it was also soothing, like placing a cold rag on a feverish forehead.

Needing to push myself further, I began to swim laps. But as I moved through the water, I could only see Violet's face.

Violet was everything I ever wanted in a woman. She was smart, gorgeous, and funny. She always kept me on my toes. She challenged and excited me. In bed, she satisfied me in ways that surpassed my wildest fantasies.

I reached the far side of the pool and climbed out, dripping water onto the tiled floor. I found a towel and wrapped myself in it.

But it was more than sex with her. It was more than the fun we had together – cooking and dancing, or even just walking along the beach, holding hands and talking. It was how I felt with her. All the bullshit fell away when I was around her. She accepted me as I was, and I damn sure didn't want her to change a bit.

I cared about Violet more than I'd ever cared about anyone.

Standing there in front of my pool, I had an epiphany. I had fallen in love with Violet Williams. I loved her! I was in love with the most beautiful, witty, incredible woman in the world.

What kind of an idiot was I to have taken this long to realize it?

I loved Violet, and now I had lost her. Thanks to my stubbornness, I'd driven off the only woman in the world for me.

And she'd probably been scared to death being contacted by the police!

Ironically, I now felt as if I were incarcerated in a prison of loneliness. But it was no less than I deserved. Violet should have gotten a prince, and I'd acted like a monster.

It was hopeless. She'd never forgive me after the horrible things I'd done.

There was nothing I could ever do to win her back.

CHAPTER 28

VIOLET

"*H*and me that box over there, please," I called out to Stuart. I was packing my things for Iowa and trying not to cry. Again.

"Let me pack that for you," Stuart said, as I attempted to put a stack of books into the box. He shook a chastising finger at me and said, "You shouldn't strain yourself like that. You need to get used to letting other people do the heavy lifting for you."

I knew he was right, but hearing the words aloud still stung. I'd always prided myself on being able to do anything I set my mind to. My independence was something I didn't like giving up, but for my baby, I was willing to make any sacrifice.

"Okay, okay. I'll go pack up my room."

I was eager to get away from all of Stuart's fussing. I knew his intentions were good, but that didn't mean he wasn't driving me crazy.

In my room, I flipped my radio on to a classic rock station. It was pathetic, but it made me feel close to Jack in some small way. I set a cardboard box on my bed and started packing things from my dresser. A picture frame, a jewelry box, some trinkets...

When I came to the beautiful pink conch shell that Jack had retrieved from the ocean at high tide, I paused. Clutching it to my chest, I broke down into sobs, unable to hold back the pain of heartbreak.

As much as I had tried not to fall for Jack McCann, I had tumbled head over heels for him. I loved him with all my heart. I loved his cocky grin and shimmering blue eyes. I loved the way he danced to the cheesiest classic rock songs without shame and even the way he sang off-key. I loved how he made me laugh and how I always felt so free when I was with him. When I was with Jack, I didn't have to pretend to be anyone but myself. He cared about the real me, and I loved him for being exactly who he was.

I froze as "Love Hurts" by Nazareth came on the radio.

How appropriate, I thought bitterly.

He'd seen so much abuse in his life, and it was a tragic irony that he had learned not to trust anyone. I was honored that he'd opened a crack in the wall around his heart and let me see the true man inside. I'd thought that meant he had healed enough to let that wall down for me forever, but that was foolish of me. I should have anticipated that getting the extortion letter from Ashley would trigger his old fears. After all the negative experiences he'd had, it was only natural for him to lash out as a way to protect himself.

I only wished he would have listened to me when I tried to explain.

Despite how much his words had hurt and angered me, I still loved him and wished him the best. I knew he'd never trust me again. I knew it was over. If we were to accidentally run into each other again, it would be too painful for both of us. It was a risk I couldn't take. I'd made the right decision to move back home to Iowa.

Most importantly, moving back home would give my child a better future. I wanted to provide the best things I could for my baby, and I didn't want to rely on Stuart's charity.

One day, when enough time had passed, I would tell Jack he had a child, but not when his emotions were still so raw. He still thought I was just using him. I needed to raise this baby on my own for a while, to prove to him it wasn't a ploy just to get money out of him.

It was a shame things had to be this way, because I knew instinctively that Jack would have made a wonderful father. He just didn't know it himself.

That thought triggered a new flood of tears. I wiped my eyes then carefully wrapped the conch shell in tissue paper and put it in the box.

I wondered if the baby would look more like me or like Jack. Either way, the child would serve as a constant reminder of the good times we'd shared and the love I had for him. I would cherish the memories forever, and one day, when the time was right, I would tell our child all about Jack.

I couldn't help but smile at the thought, and I finished packing my room as best I could without breaking down again. Just as I was finishing, a gentle knock came at my door. It was Stuart.

"Are you doing okay in here, Vi?" he asked.

"I'm all right." I tried to smile to reassure him.

"You know, you don't have to move if you don't want to. We can unpack everything and you can just stay here with me forever."

"I know," I said gratefully. "But you've already done so much for me. I don't want to be a burden to you. My parents have already cleaned out my old bedroom of storage boxes and bought a bassinet. They can't wait to help me with the baby."

"I just hate to see you trapped back in Iowa again," Stuart cried. "You were stifled there. The city is where you belong. You were truly thriving here."

"Thanks, but I can't prioritize my own needs anymore. I have to do what's best for my baby, and that means moving back home with my parents. I'll be all right. I survived there before. I can do it again." I opened my arms wide and welcomed Stuart into a heartfelt hug. I squeezed him tight, unable to keep fresh tears from streaming down my face, and said earnestly, "I'll always be grateful to you for the friendship we shared. Thank you for inviting me to come out to LA and letting me stay with you."

"I shouldn't have introduced you to Jack," Stuart said.

I shook my head. "Without you doing that, I might never have fallen in love. It doesn't matter that it didn't work out between me and Jack. The experience is something I'll always treasure."

"You're a tough cookie." Stuart smiled at me through tears of his own. He handed me a tissue and said, "I never bought into that whole it's-better-to-have-loved-and-lost thing until now. Seeing how strong you are in the face of all this is so inspiring."

"I don't know about that. So far, all I've been doing is puking and crying," I said with chagrin.

"It's okay. I've been looking for an excuse to redecorate in here," Stuart teased, and we hugged again. Stuart sniffed. "I really am going to miss you, sweetie."

"I'm going to miss you too, but going back home to Iowa really is the right thing to do. It's good for kids to have the influence of grandparents, and Mom already said she'd babysit when I get a job."

"What about your jewelry business?" Stuart blinked.

"What about it?" I shrugged. "It was a beautiful pipe dream. For a little while, it looked like it might actually come true, but then life happened and reality set in. Who knows, one day when the baby is older and doesn't need me as much, I'll be able to pick jewelry making back up again as a hobby."

"Don't throw away your dreams just because you're having a child."

"I'm not. I'm just trading one dream for another. I always wanted to be a mother, just not quite so soon. But that doesn't mean I won't dedicate a hundred percent of my attention to it."

"Okay, I won't pressure you," Stuart said, and I felt relieved he wouldn't push me about it. Sacrificing my dream of having my own jewelry business when I'd almost had it in my grasp was a disappointment unlike any other. I knew if I thought about it too much, it might morph into resentment, and I didn't want that. It was best to forget completely about it. Thinking about my baby made it easier. Having a child was worth any sacrifice, even my dream of having my own business.

Suddenly, there was the sound of a horn honking outside, and I jumped.

Stuart looked out the window and said, "The moving truck is here! Should I start loading up these boxes?"

I looked around my room, which now looked so different with boxes piled high along the walls where pictures had once hung. I wasn't just saying goodbye to this apartment, I was saying goodbye to all the hopes and dreams I'd had when I moved to LA.

Handing the first box to Stuart, I plastered a fake smile on my face and said bravely, "Yeah, let's do it. I'm ready to go back home."

CHAPTER 29

JACK

"*I* have some great news," Grayson said as he stuck his head into my office with a big grin.

"What?" I asked stoically. I could really use some good news. I hadn't been able to sleep ever since my relationship with Violet fell apart. For a while, I'd been surviving on anger, but after finding out it was Ashley who wrote that extortion letter and not Violet, I was consumed by guilt.

The guilt blended with my heartbreak, regret, and loneliness to form a pitiful soup that I'd been marinating in ever since. I knew I was acting like a complete asshole around the office, but I couldn't help it. I was too miserable on the inside not to act that way on the outside.

Grayson helped himself to the chair across from my desk and propped his feet up on my desk. Leaning back comfortably, he said, "Howard Morris is thrilled with his cybersecurity service. Ever since Maddie found the coding error in his account for that one hotel, there haven't been any problems. The system has been working flawlessly. He's ready for us to move ahead with implementing the system to the rest of his hotels across the nation. He even said he'll recommend us to all of his friends, and he's got a lot of them."

"That is great news," I said flatly. I just couldn't muster any enthusiasm for the company anymore. Lion used to mean everything to me. I lived and died for my work, but now whenever I came to the office, all I could think about was Violet's empty chair.

"What do you say we go out to the bar tonight and celebrate?"

"Forget it," I said, turning to scowl out the window.

"Obviously, it wouldn't be the bar where Ashley Stokes's sister works. Let's go to this new one I found. Every week they have all these different theme nights. There's even a classic rock night. Come on, you'll love it."

"No, thanks. I think I'll just go home tonight. I have some things to catch up on around the house."

"Are you still hung up on Violet?" Grayson asked bluntly. I could always count on my best friend to give it to me straight, with no pussyfooting around.

"She's all I can think about. I really fucked things up with her. There's no way she'll ever forgive me. Maybe I should just sell you my half of the company and go away some place far away where everything doesn't remind me of her. This office, my estate, my car, even the fucking beach all make me think of Violet and how much I love her."

"Well then, go get her back," Grayson said, as if the solution were obvious.

"Yeah, right. I'll just drive down to her place, climb her trellis like fucking Romeo, and beg her to forgive me," I scoffed.

"Why not?" Grayson said.

He made it sound so simple. I had to think long and hard to come up with a reason why it wasn't possible. In the end, I couldn't.

"Do you really think I could convince Violet to take me back?" I asked, feeling a glimmer of hope for the first time since she quit.

"Yeah, I really do," Grayson said. "I saw the way you two used to look at each other. She loved you as much as you loved her. That kind of thing doesn't just disappear over a stupid misunderstanding. Tell her you fucked up and how deeply sorry you are and see what happens. You'll never know if she'll forgive you until you try."

He got up and left, but I sat there for a long time letting his words sink in.

What if he was right? I had just assumed that there was no hope, that I had fucked up everything with Violet beyond repair.

I had to at least tell her how I felt. I had to try to win her back.

Suddenly, I was filled with energy and ideas. I ran out of the office without telling the staff I was leaving. I knew I could trust Grayson to handle things without me. I had something more important than work to take care of.

BY THE TIME I pulled up to Violet's apartment, the sun was just starting to set. There was a small moving truck parked out front, and I saw my real estate agent – Violet's roommate – loading a box into the back. I waved to him.

"Hey, Stuart!" I called out just as he was closing the back of the truck and locking it tight. "Are you moving away?"

"No," he said, sounding surprisingly snarky. With his hands on his hips, he said in a hostile tone, "Violet is."

"What? Where's she going?" I was surprised.

"None of your business," Stuart snapped rudely. "If she

wanted you to know where she was going, she'd tell you herself. Now get out of here. You've upset her enough."

"I came here to talk to her, to apologize for the way I treated her," I said, but it didn't make a difference. I watched as Stuart stomped past me, all the way up the stairs to their apartment, and slammed the door noisily behind him. I knew better than to bother knocking. It was obvious Violet had told him everything that happened between us, and he was never going to let me in.

In an odd way, I was comforted to know she had such a good friend protecting her, but that didn't mean he was going to deter me from trying to win her back.

The sun was setting fast, and it looked like Violet's moving van was loaded and ready to go. I realized she was most likely leaving for her unknown destination in the morning. If I didn't find a way to talk to her tonight, I might lose her forever.

Looking around the building, I spotted a fire escape going up the side. Even though I was over six feet tall, I had to jump to grab the bottom rung. I missed the first time but caught it on the second and lowered the ladder so I could climb up.

"Shit, my flowers!" I cried out as I nearly forgot the bouquet of violets I'd purchased from the florist on my way over. Once I had them firmly in hand, I began to climb the rickety ladder. It creaked under my weight, but it held, and I climbed to the second floor, to her apartment.

"Violet Williams, I'm sorry!" I shouted out loudly toward the window.

"Jack?" Violet appeared at the window and opened it quickly. She leaned out and frowned at me. "What are you doing here?"

"I came to tell you how sorry I am," I said earnestly. "I acted like a complete asshole. You didn't deserve to be treated like that."

"You got that right," Violet said, glaring.

"I love you," I shouted out frantically.

"What?" she whispered as she stared at me with her eyes wide.

"I love you, Violet, with all my heart."

She stared at me for a long moment. I thought she was going to slam the window shut. But instead, she opened her mouth.

"I love you too," she finally said, and her eyes brimmed with tears. But just as suddenly, the light in her eyes turned cold, as if a switch had been flipped, and the tears in her eyes fell down her cheeks as if in sorrow. She wiped at them with the back of her hand and said softly, "Sometimes love isn't enough, especially when there's more at stake than just you and me."

It was a cryptic thing to say, but I realized she must have been referring to Ashley and the letter. Speaking urgently, before she closed the window again, I knew I had to convince her not to go.

"You're right. I want to tell you how extremely sorry I am for the way I behaved. It's not enough for me to love you. You deserve a man who will respect and listen to you. Someone who will trust and believe in you and who will always have your back. Please accept my apology for not treating you that way from the beginning. I promise to be the man you deserve from now until the day I die."

"Does this mean you no longer think I'm a gold digger?" she asked skeptically.

"Accusing you of writing that extortion letter was the worst mistake I've ever made. I should have listened to you when you tried to tell me about Ashley. I should have believed you when you said it wasn't you. I was a fool and a complete jerk. I've regretted every moment since it happened. Please, forgive me."

There was a long pause as Violet looked thoughtfully out the window. My heart pounded behind my ribs like a scared animal trapped in a cage. Finally, she spoke.

"I accept your apology, but I can't come back to you," Violet said, lifting my heart only to drop it again.

"Why not?"

"You're too late," she said simply. "I'm leaving for Iowa in the morning."

"Don't go," I cried out. Now was the time to throw away all my pride, to be brutally honest about my feelings. "Don't give up on us, Violet. What we have is special. One of a kind. We can't throw that away."

"But you never wanted a commitment," she said quietly.

I shook my head. "I was a fool to think that. I only want you, no one else. And I don't only want sex, I want all of you, Violet. Nothing in my life has any meaning if you're not there to share it with me. You're the only thing that matters anymore. Please, come back to me."

Violet was silent for what felt like an eternity, but I knew better than to push her. I gave her the space she needed to think.

Finally, she looked at me and held out her hand, welcoming me into her window.

"Come inside," she said softly. "We need to talk. You might not want me back after you hear what I have to say."

"There's nothing you could ever do or say that would make me love you any less," I vowed. My heart was soaring. She was at least willing to talk to me.

"Don't be so sure," Violet said.

CHAPTER 30

VIOLET

"*W*hat is it you want to tell me?" Jack asked with an expression of eager anticipation.

I realized in that moment I didn't have the slightest idea how to begin.

Learning that I was pregnant was undoubtedly going to come as a shock to him. We'd been so careful, using a condom every time. He might not even believe my news. Or he might accuse me of using the pregnancy to get money out of him.

Worst of all, learning the truth could make him stop loving me. He'd been very clear that he never wanted to be a father.

Well, if that was going to be the case, it was better to find out now. I couldn't bear getting back together with him just to have my heart broken later.

There was no putting it off any longer. My moving truck was packed, and I was leaving for Iowa in the morning. The man I loved was standing on my fire escape asking me to come back to him. It was now or never.

But as my heart pounded in my chest, I found it difficult to speak.

This could be it. He could choose to abandon me now. I wasn't sure I could survive the pain of losing him again.

I sat on the edge of my bed and patted the mattress next to me. Fidgeting with my hands in my lap, I swallowed down the lump in my throat. "You should sit down for this," I said hoarsely.

He looked at me, and his eyes had that spark in them I loved so much. It was the same spark that appeared whenever he had a genius idea at work or was fired up about something. It lit up his face when he laughed or danced. That spark, that bright shining light of passion and life, filled his eyes and illuminated my world whenever we were together. It was what made me love him and how I knew he loved me.

It saddened me to realize that after I told him my secret, I might never see that spark again.

Still, it had to be done. He'd laid his heart out for me. I had to tell him the truth and then live with the consequences.

"You're really building up the anticipation on this," Jack teased in a failed attempt to lighten the tension in the air. Taking my hand, he said gently, "Just say it. Whatever you have to tell me can't be that big a deal. I love you, and nothing is going to change that."

Drawing in a deep breath, I said it quickly.

"I'm pregnant."

It took a moment for my words to register in Jack's mind – a very long moment. Time seemed to stretch out forever.

When those two words finally dawned on him, his eyes grew wide, and his complexion turned ghostly white.

CHAPTER 31

"*Y*ou're pregnant?" I asked in a raspy voice, and Violet nodded.

She began talking so quickly, I could hardly understand a word she said.

"Don't worry, I'm going to do this all on my own, Jack. I don't want anything from you. You don't have to be involved in the baby's life if you don't want to be."

I was stunned into silence, too shocked to know how to respond.

"That's why I'm moving to Iowa," she continued. "I can send you pictures if you want. But if you don't, you'll never have to hear from me again."

Hearing her say those words shook me from my trance. I spoke before I even knew what I was going to say.

"Don't go. Don't take our baby to Iowa," I said, the words surprising both of us. "I love you, Violet. I don't want to be without you, no matter what. And if you're having our baby, then I want all three of us to be a family together."

Tears filled her eyes, and she gripped my hands with hers.

Blinking back her tears, she stubbornly refused to let them fall.

"I love you too," she said, "but raising a baby together will mean changing your entire life. Are you really sure you want to commit to doing this with me?"

I thought about my entire life in the flash of a moment — the struggles, the fear, the abuse from Dad, and how I never wanted to be like him. I thought of the rise of my company, the money and fame, the partying in bars and having women throw themselves at me, the sports cars and beach houses, and all the extravagances of my life. I thought of the loneliness, of never having anyone by my side to share it all with, both the highs and the lows, and how none of it meant anything if I was empty inside.

I thought of Violet and how she had changed everything. She wasn't just my assistant at work, she was my best friend and my lover. She was the first person I wanted to see when I woke up and the last one I wanted to talk to at night when I fell asleep. With Violet, I no longer wanted to be alone. She had already become my family, and when I was with her, I knew I was home.

So, why shouldn't we bring a baby into the world and become a real family? With Violet by my side, I could be the father I'd always wished I'd had as a child. She made me a better man, and I had no doubt she'd help me be a good parent. I could already tell she'd be a phenomenal mother.

I pulled Violet into my arms and held her to me so that our hearts were beating together as one. Gazing into her eyes, I decided to be brutally honest and speak straight from my heart.

"I never wanted to be a father," I began haltingly. Violet drew in her breath, wincing, and I continued before she could interrupt. "But hearing that you're carrying my child, I can see a wonderful future together where I'm able to give my wife and child all the love and support I never had."

"Really?" Violet swallowed, and I saw a tear escape the corner of her eye.

I caught it on my finger as I caressed her cheek. I brought it to my lips and kissed it, making the tear disappear. Then, I knelt down on one knee. Violet gasped.

"Violet Williams, I love you with all my heart and soul. I'm proud to be the father of our child, and I want us to be together as a family. Will you do me the honor of marrying me?"

"Yes! A million times, yes!" Violet wept openly. I leapt up and pulled her into my arms, twirling her around the room joyously, making her squeal with happiness. Then, I set her down and kissed her with all the passion and love I felt deep inside. She returned the embrace and the kiss, nearly taking my breath away, as we held each other, laughing and weeping with joy.

"Is everything all right in here?" Stuart broke into the room looking worried and a little out of breath. He was surprised to see me there, but then he noticed the open window, and it quickly made sense.

"Yes, everything is more than fine," Violet cried out exuberantly. "I'm engaged, Stuart!"

Stuart's eyes moved from Violet to me. His skepticism was obvious.

"Are you sure about this, Violet?" he asked.

"I'm sure," she said. "I was wrong about everything. This is what I want, what I've always wanted."

Stuart looked at us a moment and then his face broke out in a grin. "Well, then, congratulations! I'm so happy for you two!" He hugged her tight, but then he pulled back with a pouty expression.

"What's wrong?" I asked.

"I just realized this means I loaded that moving truck for nothing," he said. "Now I'll have to unpack it all."

"Leave it packed," I said. "We'll take it to my house. My new fiancée and our baby will be living there from now on."

Stuart raised his eyebrows.

"Don't think that just because we're engaged, you can start bossing me around and telling me what to do," Violet said with a smile.

"I would never think that," I said with a laugh, thrilled that Violet was back to being her regular feisty self – and that I was lucky enough to be having a baby with her.

CHAPTER 32

"*D*oes my belly show under my dress?" I asked, feeling terribly self-conscious now that I had entered the second trimester of my pregnancy.

"A little, but it only makes you look more beautiful," my mom said as she helped me put on my veil. The layers of delicate tulle flowed around me like a waterfall. My hair was pinned up in a sweep of curls that had taken the hairdresser nearly two hours to design, and the white satin gown I wore made me feel feminine and beautiful. I hugged my mom and said gratefully, "Thank you for letting me wear your dress."

"When I married your father thirty years ago, I'd always hoped one day I'd be able to watch my own daughter wear it for her own wedding. Jessica wanted a new dress, but I'm so glad you asked to wear mine."

"I'm glad the seamstress was able to let it out enough to accommodate my belly." I grinned, still feeling self-conscious about my growing size.

The doctor said my weight was increasing at a normal rate and the baby was healthy and doing well. I just couldn't believe how much I already loved and worried about him.

We'd just found out the sex at our last appointment, and Jack had been overjoyed we were having a son. He was already making a list of names. I saw it on his computer at work, even though he tried to hide it.

"Aren't you supposed to be working on writing your vows?" I'd teased him.

"That's already done," he'd said with a kiss. Then he arched a brow at me playfully and said, "How about yours? Are you finished writing your vows?"

"Not yet," I confessed, but I already knew in my heart what I wanted to say.

We both wanted to get married on the beach with the sun setting in front of us, in a small ceremony with just family and friends. Dad said he already felt that Jack was like a son. Grayson would undoubtedly be Jack's best man, but I had a tough choice for my maid of honor. Should I go with Maddie or Stuart? In the end, I knew in my heart that I had to go with my sister.

Jessica cried when I asked her, and I lightened the mood by joking, "Don't get too emotional. I just picked you because you're two months further along in your pregnancy than I am. I figure I won't look so enormous if I stand next to you."

"You say that now, but you're going to love having a baby belly and feeling your child kick for the first time. There's no greater feeling," Jessica said, and she'd been right.

Even now, with my belly looming under my wedding dress, I couldn't help but wrap my arms around my stomach in a loving embrace, protecting and hugging my unborn baby. I felt him kick as if in response, and it made my heart swell with joy.

"It's time for the ceremony," my father said. He entered the tent where I'd been getting ready with Mom and Jessica by my side. Dad looked dashing in the tuxedo Jack had purchased for him, and I marveled that this was one of the few times I'd seen my father in something other than a plaid shirt.

I heard the music begin. I watched as Jessica's husband escorted Mom out of the tent as "Somewhere Over the Rainbow" played on a ukulele. Next, Jessica walked down the aisle in the sand, carrying a bouquet of beautiful tropical flowers.

"This is it!" I beamed at my father, and my heart began to pound as the ukulele music turned into "Here Comes the Bride." I took my father's arm and drew in a breath as we walked toward the altar made of driftwood and covered in seashells and tropical flowers.

My gaze focused on Jack standing there in his tuxedo, looking incredibly handsome and sexy. His face was filled with so much love that I felt tears come to my eyes. Suddenly, I was overcome with gratitude to have found him.

I was marrying a man who loved me beyond my wildest dreams. I loved him just as much in return.

Jack recited his vows, and his beautiful words took my breath away.

"I came to life the day I met you," he said as our family and friends listened around us and the ocean waves lapped in the background. "Now, our combined love grows within you, a new life that is half you and half me. I promise to spend the rest of my days doing everything I can to be the father and husband you both deserve, and to make you as happy as you've made me."

He slipped the ring onto my finger. It was a splendid band comprised of platinum and gold strands interwoven like our very lives.

Now, it was my turn to recite the vows I had composed, and I could feel the eyes of all our family and friends upon me. Suddenly, my throat went dry, and I had to focus on looking directly at Jack to keep from losing my nerve.

"I didn't come to California looking to find love. I came to prove my independence and that I didn't need a husband or children to be happy," I began. There were light chuckles from those who knew me best. "Then, I met you, and everything changed. Now I can't wait to be a wife and a mother, only I realize I don't have to give up my independence to do it. We make each other whole and complete, two separate strands that come together in perfect unison. I love you, Jack McCann. I'm so blessed to spend the rest of my life by your side."

I slipped the ring onto Jack's finger. It was an identical twin to the ring he gave me, only larger. Our eyes met, and I felt all his love for me.

Then, the officiate smiled and said, "I now pronounce you husband and wife. You may kiss the bride!"

Our family and friends erupted into cheers, but I didn't hear them. The only thing I was aware of was Jack's mouth over mine as we kissed each other passionately.

The party lasted late into the night, with plenty of food and dancing to satisfy all. When finally the last guest had left, Jack and I walked back up the path from the beach to the house, hand in hand for the first time as a married couple.

I wrapped my arms around Jack's strong neck as he lifted me into his arms and carried me across the threshold. My lips found his, and I kissed him long and hard until we reached the bedroom and he laid me gently upon the bed.

"I love you, Mrs. McCann," he said with a sexy grin. I pulled him onto the bed beside me.

"I love you too," I said. I began unbuttoning the many buttons of his tuxedo shirt as he set to work unfastening the hooks of my bridal gown.

It was like unwrapping a package, as we each delighted in peeling away the layers of each other's clothing until we were both naked. It was the first time Jack had seen my baby bump in the flesh since we'd decided to abstain from sex in the weeks before our wedding to heighten the romance.

"You are so beautiful," Jack whispered in awe. He brought his lips to kiss me all over my rounded belly. His hands found my breasts and massaged them sensuously before he brought his mouth upon them, kissing his way toward my sensitive nipples in slow circles. When his mouth closed over my nipples, gently flicking them with his tongue, I threw back my head and moaned with pleasure.

"I want you inside me," I panted, and I reached for his cock. He was already hard, and I delighted in stroking him with my hands, driving him to suckle my breasts with increasing passion.

"Not yet," Jack whispered. "I want to taste you first."

He parted my legs and kissed me over my sensitive folds, gradually increasing the tension as he lapped at me in a tight rhythm. The pleasure was incredible. I gripped his hair, gyrating against his mouth as he held my hips. He drove me wild with desire until finally my body writhed with ecstasy and my orgasm consumed me.

I caught my breath, coming down from the throes of bliss, and he caressed me gently. I clutched him, pulling him toward me hungrily.

"Now! I want you now!" I panted. Jack willingly obliged, and I sighed with pleasure at the feel of his huge cock filling my wet and ready opening.

I wrapped my arms and legs around him, holding him to me as we pulsed and thrust in perfect rhythm, undulating together in perfect symmetry, the two becoming one.

I could feel the orgasm rising from deep within me, and I clutched and clung to him, wanting this moment to last forever. His tongue plunged deep within my mouth, and the kiss made my body open up even more to receive him into my depths. My hands ran over his strong, chiseled body. His muscles tightened as he thrust more quickly in the final moment before he released.

"Come for me, Jack," I whispered.

He moaned and then shuddered and convulsed as he came deep within me. I clenched my legs around him, squeezing him tighter. He closed his eyes in ecstasy.

The sensation of his cock throbbing inside my walls pushed me over the edge, and I orgasmed with him, my entire body exploding with the most intense pleasure I'd ever felt in all the times we'd made love before.

We'd always had amazing sexual chemistry together, but this was the first time we'd made love as husband and wife. It was more incredible than any of the times that had preceded it. This feeling came from intimacy and love and knowing that we were now connected to each other forever in the bonds of matrimony.

"I love you, my wife," Jack murmured as his climax subsided and we lay together in the bed, just holding each other close.

"I love you too, my husband," I said, and I placed his hand on my belly so he could feel our baby kicking.

We were a family, now and forever.

EPILOGUE

JACK

I opened the front door to see Stuart standing there with a big grin on his face. He was decked out in a Hawaiian shirt and bright coral shorts.

"Hey, stranger!" he joked.

"Long time no see, Stuart." I chuckled. It'd just been a few days since he'd been over. Now that the weather was warming up, our beach house had been a popular spot with our friends.

He gave me a brotherly hug. We'd long since buried the hatchet after the misunderstanding between Violet and me. Stuart was an important part of our lives. He waltzed into the beach house carrying a gift wrapped in brightly colored paper.

"Hey, Stuart!" Violet called. "We're in the living room."

We joined the small gathering in the sunlight-filled room that overlooked the ocean. Everyone welcomed Stuart – Grayson, Maddie, and Violet's parents, who had flown in for a visit.

"Everyone's talking about your jewelry, Violet!" Stuart said as he added his gift to the pile on a table to the side. "My coworkers all want to place more orders with you, but they say you're booked for months!"

"She's swamped with customers," Violet's dad said proudly. "Didn't you say you had a bunch of orders from Europe now?"

Violet nodded. "My earrings are selling like hotcakes!"

"The company's growing so fast. It's time for you to expand," I said as I looked at Violet. "You should hire more employees to handle the admin work. And you need to train a couple workers to help make the pieces."

"That's not for you to say, mister," Violet said playfully with mock anger. "Made With Love Jewelry is my company to run the way I see fit. You've got Lion, Inc., to take care of."

"You're right. I'm just so proud of you, I get excited," I said with a smile. "Do you have any idea how long it took me and Grayson to achieve the level of success you're already reaching?"

"Well, the money I save by not having a brick-and-mortar store and selling my jewelry strictly online is the reason my profits are so high," Violet said modestly.

I loved how humble she still was. But I knew her success had more to do with her talent for design than her business practices.

Her jewelry was now highly sought after. She'd even been getting some orders from Hollywood's most elite celebrities. Especially after an actress announced she was wearing Violet's jewelry at the Oscars, her sales had soared. Yet Violet was still the same down-to-earth Midwest girl I loved, with her fresh smile and her sassy wit.

"Plus, I have the best programmer in California running my website," she added with a sly smile.

"That's true," I agreed. "And I may never forgive you for stealing Maddie away from me. Especially after I already lost a great assistant when your company started taking off," I teased.

She gave me a guilty look, and I placed a tender kiss on her lips to prove there was nothing but love between us.

Maddie laughed along with our other friends and said, "Hey, I told Violet long ago I would go with her if she landed a job at a great company. And Made With Love Jewelry is the best there is."

"Don't worry, buddy, I'll never leave you," Grayson said. He put his arm around my shoulders, and we all laughed lightheartedly.

Suddenly, Violet's mother interrupted the socializing. She came into the room with a sleepy-eyed boy in her arms.

"Look who's finally awake from his nap," she crooned. "It's the birthday boy!"

Dylan stretched out his arms toward me with eager excitement, and I proudly hugged my son close to my chest as Violet stroked his fine hair. He had my brown hair color and her violet-gray eyes. Of course, I was partial, but he was definitely the cutest baby I'd ever seen. And everyone agreed.

"Hi, birthday boy!" Violet said as he gave his mother a hug, burying his face against her chest.

I could hardly believe it had been an entire year since Dylan had been born. Impossible as it seemed, I loved the little guy more and more with each passing day.

Fatherhood was an even greater joy than I had hoped it would be.

"Are you ready for cake, Dylan?" Violet set him on his feet, still holding his hand. His sleepiness was soon replaced by excitement.

Watching my son toddle on wobbly legs toward his first birthday cake made my heart swell.

The only thing that came close to the way I felt when I was with him was the love I felt for his mother.

Violet got a lot of teasing on social media for removing LA's "Sexiest CEO Bachelor" from the market. But I'd never been happier in my life than I was being her husband. Violet was the best wife and mother a man could ask for, and I was grateful every day that she'd agreed to marry me.

Surrounded by our friends and family, I held her hand joyfully as everyone sang "Happy Birthday" to Dylan. We watched as he tentatively dug his fists into the slice of chocolate cake we set before him on his highchair.

He wasn't sure what to do with the gooey mess at first. But when a piece of it managed to make it into his mouth, his eyes grew wide, and his chubby arms flailed excitedly. After that first taste of sugar, the toddler quickly figured out how to get fistfuls of cake into his mouth, not to mention all over his hair and his adorable face.

"I don't think I've ever seen anyone enjoy their birthday cake quite so much in my entire life," I mused as I held Violet to me.

When no one was looking, I nibbled her ear lovingly. She was so beautiful whenever she gazed at our son, I couldn't resist kissing her.

"Me neither," Violet giggled softly. "It's got me thinking, though. Your birthday is next month, Jack. What can I possibly make for you that will make you nearly so happy?"

I held her to me and kissed her with all the love in my heart.

"I know," I said with a grin. "How about a daughter?"

Thank you for reading! If you liked this book, you'll LOVE Boss Daddy.

One wild night with Grant changed my life.
I thought he was gone forever.
Until I meet my new next-door neighbor.

Grant's hotter than ever.
And he just saw me wearing nothing but a towel.

He wants to start over.
Pick up where we left off.
But there's something he doesn't know yet.

I have a six-year-old secret.
And she has Grant's blue eyes.

This full-length romance is a fun, sexy, and heart-warming read.
You'll fall in love with Grant and Ada, and you'll adore their
happily ever after!

Grab your copy of Boss Daddy here!

SNEAK PEEK OF BOSS DADDY!

ABOUT THE BOOK

One wild night with Grant changed my life forever.
Never thought I'd see him again...
Until I meet my new neighbor.

Seven years ago, I sat next to a gorgeous man in first class.
The flight was a bumpy ride...
But that was NOTHING compared to what I gave him later.

No regrets.
Except for one.
I didn't get his contact info.

Now he's my sexy next-door neighbor.
And he just saw me wearing nothing but a towel.

He wants to start over.
Pick up where we left off.

But there's something he doesn't know yet.

**I have a six-year-old secret with Grant's blue eyes.
And she needs her daddy more than anything...
If he'll step up to the plate.**

Grab your copy of Boss Daddy here!

CHAPTER ONE: ADA

"*E*xcuse me? Miss?"

"Huh?" I started and blinked my eyes, the bright airport terminal coming back into focus.

A woman with blonde streaks in her hair glared at me, her eyes narrowed. Sitting up straighter, I wiped drool from the corner of my mouth. How long had I been asleep?

The woman folded her arms. "Do you mind putting away your..." She cleared her throat and lowered her voice. "Penis hat?"

"My..." In question, I lifted a hand to my head.

That's right! My penis hat. Bright pink and fuzzy, it was really a headband, not a hat. Two pink penises protruded from the top of it. From far away, one might think it was the head part of a bunny costume.

"There are children all around." Blondie nodded at two children sitting next to her. Neither one of them seemed to notice me or anyone else, as their noses were buried in tablets.

Still. Falling asleep in an airport while wearing leftover bachelorette party paraphernalia hadn't been my intention. I hadn't even meant to wear the headband. I'd been going through my suitcase after my flight was canceled, looking for deodorant, when half of my belongings tumbled from the bag. I'd put the headband on, merely intending to hold it there and free my hands for a minute.

"Sorry." My face warming, I removed the headband.

Her lips pursed. "Hm. It must be nice to not have kids to worry about."

I opened my mouth, but since I wasn't sure how to respond to that, closed it. I could be rude back, but what was the point?

Instead of stashing the headband back in my suitcase, I walked over to a trashcan and tossed it. Something told me that it would fail to become a cherished, nostalgic wedding token.

Which was too bad. Wasn't I supposed to feel different following my one and only sister's wedding?

I tried. I really did. When Nicole announced her engagement, I was happy for her, albeit a little hurt.

She already had a family in Los Angeles. Meaning me, now that our parents were gone. Why had she needed to move to Philadelphia to start a new family and leave me behind?

Shaking off thoughts of my sister, I returned to my seat. A dull ache had started in my temples, and I felt like I could sleep for twelve hours straight.

Unfortunately, that wasn't going to happen. The four days on the East Coast for the wedding had severely set me back when it came to both school and shifts at the sushi restaurant where I waitressed. I was a month away from graduating with a journalism degree, and I had exams to study for.

Nicole knew how hard it had been for me to make the wedding. That was why she had footed the bill for my plane tickets and bridesmaid's dress. The timing wasn't great for me, but I'd pushed aside my concerns and hopped on a plane to Philadelphia with high hopes.

For a while there, leading up to the wedding week, I had actually thought things were changing with her. That after several years of barely talking, she would welcome me back with open arms.

It wasn't so. All week long, at the rehearsal dinner, bachelorette party, and ceremony, my older sister hardly spoke to me. It was all about her friends.

I tried not to be hurt that she had chosen a girl she'd only known for a year as her maid of honor. Tried not to be hurt when she barely mentioned me in her rehearsal dinner speech. And not a word about our parents.

As the week dragged on, it became increasingly clear that Nicole might have invited me to her wedding out of a sense of obligation and nothing else. Which hurt more than anything. Well, except for that one thing.

"Adaline Jones," a voice cut with static said.

I yelped and jumped. "That's me."

"Paging Adaline Jones," the woman said again. "This is the last call for Flight 274 to LAX."

"Oh my God," I breathed.

Zipping past the trash can, I darted around a stroller and jumped over the outstretched legs of a sleeping man. I nearly face-planted avoiding a small dog in a carrying case.

Suitcase in hand, I barreled toward the gate. A bored-looking woman blinked at me.

"Adaline Jones?"

"That's me." I presented my ticket, still trying to catch my breath.

"I've been calling you for ten minutes."

"Sorry." I cringed. "I didn't hear you."

"Go on." She scanned my ticket and waved me through. "We were just about to close the doors."

"Thank you!" Picking up my carry-on, I jogged for the plane.

My original flight back home had been canceled several hours ago, and that meant I would now get in even later than I hoped for. So much for catching up on schoolwork tonight. Tomorrow would be a late night.

But hey, at least I'd woken up in time to catch this flight.

Thanks, Blondie.

At the plane's door, I inspected my ticket. Seat B2. First class.

"Wait." I turned around, addressing no one in particular.

This ticket couldn't be for me. I'd never flown first class a day in my life. That seemed akin to flying back to California on a unicorn.

"Ma'am. Let's go, please." A stewardess with a fake smile gestured for me to enter the plane.

"Right. Sorry."

I entered the first-class area of the plane and looked around nervously. Curtains separated the spacious rows, and the windows were larger here. It only took a few steps to reach my row.

In the aisle seat, a man with light brown hair and blue eyes frowned at his phone. At the sight of him, my heart jumped.

"Excuse me," I said.

He finished typing a text before looking up. Instead of saying anything, he merely blinked at me. Long lashes swept dangerously close to his high cheekbones, making my breath catch in my throat.

First, I get upgraded to first class, and then I get to sit next to this hunk? This day was turning out to be much better than anticipated.

"That's my seat." I pointed at the window seat next to him.

"You don't say?" His deep voice carried a hint of a growl. "So you're the one who held up the plane?"

"That's me." I grinned wide, hoping he was trying to be funny.

Opening up the hatch above his head, I stuffed my suitcase in. It didn't fit perfectly, so I had to hit it a few times. With each hit, my torso shook. Which meant my breasts jiggled.

Dropping my arms, I caught him looking at my chest. The second he saw me watching him, though, he dropped his gaze.

"There. We're held up no longer. Excuse me." I turned to the side, giving him my back as I side-stepped to the window seat.

He leaned away from me, his chin propped in his hand. From the way he was acting, you would think I smelled like garbage.

Wait. Did I smell like garbage? Last night, after Oliver and Nicole drove off in their car with "Just Married" painted on the back, I helped myself to another drink at the bar. Then another.

And maybe one more, for good measure.

The end result was falling asleep the second I reached my hotel. In the morning, I had time to jump in the shower for no more than a minute before dashing off to the airport. It was entirely plausible that I had missed a spot or two.

I lifted the hem of my T-shirt and gave it a sniff. Nope. I seemed to smell good, like shampoo and the coconut-scented body wash that had been in the hotel room.

The flight attendant went down the aisle, closing all the baggage compartments. The plane shuddered to life, and I leaned back into the soft seat, my hands clutching the armrests. Take-off was always the hardest part.

"I hope it was worth it."

"What was that?" I looked at the man next to me. This close up, I could see that he was in either his late twenties or early thirties, his skin smooth and dark stubble dotting his jaw.

Something rolled through my belly, an urge that made it hard to look away from him.

"I hope that whatever you were doing," he said, "was worth delaying everyone on this flight for."

I huffed. Okay. So he was trying to be a dick. Or it was his modus operandi? Maybe he was this way with everyone all the time.

I lifted my chin. "In fact, yes. I was helping someone who needed it."

"Oh, really?" He arched a thick eyebrow. "Who?"

"A child." My heart raced, as it always did when I lied. "A disabled child."

One corner of his lips turned up into a smirk. "Is that why you had that phallic headband on?"

My jaw dropped. He saw me in the airport?

He looked away from me. "Don't be flattered. You were sleeping with your suitcase right in the middle of the walkway. I had to step over it to get past. It was hard not to notice you."

"People can sleep in airports. They do it all the time."

"I'm sure they do."

I took a deep breath and clenched my jaw. Judging by his expensive watch, his perfectly fitted suit, the fact that he was in first class, and his snotty attitude, I got the distinct sense that he had never slept in an airport terminal.

Must be nice.

"I'm sorry," I hissed. "Not everyone has an all-access pass to the VIP lounge."

He picked up his phone and started tapping away at it. "Thank God for that."

A disgruntled sound escaped my throat. Out of all the people on this plane, I had to sit next to a stuck-up jerk.

I craned my neck, looking for the flight attendant. Maybe it wasn't too late to switch seats.

She came down the aisle, pointing at people and telling them to switch off devices or buckle up.

"Excuse me." I raised my hand as I stood up halfway.

"Have a seat, please." She smiled in her tight way.

"I just need—"

"Is it an emergency?"

I half dropped my hand. "Um, no. I was wondering if I could change seats."

"Yes," the man next to me breathed. "That would be delightful."

"I'm sorry," the flight attendant said. "There are no more seats available. It's a fully booked flight."

"Maybe someone would like to switch with—"

"Buckle up, please," she interrupted, walking away before she even finished talking.

Defeated, I dropped into my seat and buckled up.

The man chuckled. It was a deep bass, sending vibrations into my belly and stirring up an excitement it shouldn't have. I hated him all the more for it.

He turned to me, a self-satisfied smirk on his lips. "As much as I would have loved to get rid of you, I must admit that it felt good to watch you be turned down."

I stuck my tongue out at him, not caring how immature it made me look. I pulled the blinds down on the window and stared straight ahead.

The next six hours on the plane were already starting to look like hell.

CHAPTER TWO: GRANT

Don't look at her. Don't look at her.

Despite the sound advice running through my head, I peeked at the young woman sitting next to me. She'd drawn the window blinds and turned her overhead light on, giving me enough visibility to study her.

Rich chocolate-brown hair falling in layers around her shoulders and down her back. Big brown eyes with dark lashes. Full lips. Jeans that hugged her hips, and a tight T-shirt with an oversized corduroy jacket. On the thinner side, but with breasts large enough to fill my palms.

Stifling a groan, I looked away. Usually, I didn't chide myself for lusting after women. If I saw someone I liked, I approached her and started small talk. More often than not, women were more than willing to spend more time with me.

Not this one. She looked at me like I'd ridden in on a horse from hell. Which meant attempting to get friendly with her would be a waste of time.

She was a tough one. A firecracker to the nth degree. That much had become apparent as soon as she opened her mouth.

Out of the corner of my eye, I saw her reach into the flap on the seat in front of her and pull out the menu. She pressed a finger to her lips, perusing it. Pearly white teeth bit down on her lower lip, and my cock twitched to life.

Tearing my gaze from her, I adjusted myself in the seat. First class had always felt so roomy. Not anymore.

She put the menu back in the sleeve.

"Not getting anything?" I asked.

"No. Just looking."

From her light jacket's pocket, she pulled a small paper-back. It had been rolled up so that the worn cover was bent. Judging by its condition, it had been around for decades.

The cover photo, that of a shirtless man with a buxom redhead clinging to him, confirmed my suspicion. The romance novel looked like it was from the eighties.

Feeling my gaze, she looked up. "Yes?"

"Interesting reading choice."

Her expression soured. "What's that supposed to mean?"

"Nothing. I was only making a comment."

Shit. What the hell was wrong with me? Of course I was making a comment! That's what you do when you open your mouth and something other than a question comes out.

Usually, I wasn't this disoriented. Something about this woman, with her bright eyes and crackling energy, made me dumb. She made me want to stay on this plane when it landed in LA. Forget going back to my restaurant chain.

Leaving Lucas, my old college buddy in Philly, always put me in a funk. It made me want to play hooky from the job I usually loved so much.

The vixen next to me made the feeling worse. I wanted to hijack the plane and take it to a private island where it could drop me and Little Miss Sassy Pants off. An island where we could spend days and nights stretched out on the sand, my hands exploring every dip and curve of her body...

Closing my eyes, I forced myself to stop. I was only driving myself wild.

This woman wasn't even pleasant, for God's sake. It had merely been far too long since I'd seen action, and she was unbelievably hot.

On second thought, no, it hadn't been that long. But the last woman I had been with paled in comparison to the one sitting next to me. In fact, it was hard to believe anyone could hold a candle to her.

She had gone back to staring at her romance novel, although I could tell she wasn't reading. Her eyes weren't moving across the page.

"Look," I said, "I'm sorry if I came off the wrong way."

Her head cocked at that. Slowly, she put the book down and turned to me. "Thank you. I appreciate that."

I inclined my head. "The drink cart is on its way. Can I buy you a drink to make up for my poor behavior?"

Her full lips smirked. "The first-class drinks are complimentary."

"How do you know that?"

She pointed at the menu she had perused earlier. A second later, she scowled. "Do you think I've never been in first class before?"

"Have you?"

"I, well, no, but that..." She tucked silky hair behind an ear, her frustration mounting and somehow making her even cuter. "You were trying to impress me by pretending to buy me a drink, weren't you?"

I checked a sigh. "No. I wasn't. Will you please have a drink with me? That's all I wanted. We're stuck on this plane for hours and a little company would be nice."

Her shoulders dropped, the defenses going down. "Yeah, it would be nice."

"Thank you. What would you like?" The stewardess and her bar cart had almost reached us.

"Gin and tonic. Thank you."

"Two Nolets and tonic," I told the stewardess.

We waited silently while she made our drinks, and it seemed the air between us buzzed with a kinetic energy. This woman, whose name I didn't even know, was stealing all of my attention.

With our drinks prepared, I passed her one and raised the other in a toast. "To the flight."

"To the flight." She clinked her glass against mine then pressed it to her lips. Heat roared below my belt.

I took a slow slip, enjoying the top-shelf gin. For an airplane cocktail, first class or not, it was pretty decent.

"I don't even know your name."

"Oh, you don't, do you?" She took another sip. It became clear she wasn't about to tell me what it was.

"Are you going to make me guess? Because if you're playing a game, I should warn you who you're dealing with. I'm very good at coming out on top."

Her cheeks turned pink. I hadn't meant for the "on top" part to be suggestive, but I wouldn't have gone back and changed the word choice if I could.

She looked down, then flicked her gaze back up to mine. "It's Rochelle."

"Rochelle?" I tested the word out, letting it rest heavy on my tongue. A nice name, but it didn't suit her. "Funny. You don't look like a Rochelle."

Her chin lifted in defiance. "Well, my parents couldn't exactly look into the future and see what I would one day look like."

I raised my eyebrows. "True."

Time to take another long sip. It seemed I couldn't say the right thing.

Rochelle sighed. "I'm sorry. You apologized to me, and I shouldn't be acting this rude. It's just that I'm stressed right now. It was an annoying week, and I have a lot to do when I get home." She waved her hand dismissively. "Will you accept my apology?"

I leaned close to her, so that our faces were only inches apart. "With zero hesitation."

It would have been difficult to miss her quick inhale. Her pupils dilated, and her lips parted ever so slightly.

"So, Rochelle." I leaned back into my own space. Time to give her a breather. "What do you do?"

"I'm a student. In my senior year."

"Congratulations." She was a tad younger than I had pegged her. I didn't usually go for younger women, but it wasn't a deal-breaker.

"What about you? You live in LA?"

"Yes, I own a business with multiple locations."

"That sounds busy." Her lips puckered around her drink's tiny black straw, and I was hit with a vision of her doing the same with my cock.

I cleared my throat. "It is demanding."

"Were you staring at my lips?"

I weighed the possible answers. "What if," I finally and slowly said, "I was?"

She didn't get the chance to answer. The plane pitched, spilling our drinks and making several people scream. One of them was Rochelle. Her free hand grabbed onto my forearm with a vise grip, and she sucked in a shuddering breath.

Instantly, my body was on high alert, adrenaline pumping through it. "It's all right. It's only turbulence."

I put my hand on hers, stopping myself from wrapping both arms around her and pulling her onto my lap, like I really wanted to do.

A voice came over the intercom. "Ladies and gentlemen, this is your captain speaking. As you just felt, we're hitting some turbulence. It'll be bumpy for the next hour or so. Fasten your seat belts and hang tight."

Rochelle let out a guttural moan. "I hate turbulence."

"It's not fun, but I like to think of it as a ride. Just pretend you're at a theme park."

She twisted her lips. "I don't think that will work for me."

"So what will work, then?"

"I can only think of one thing." She downed what was left of her gin and tonic in one gulp.

I raised two fingers to get the stewardess' attention. As

soon as it was safe for her to serve again, we would need another round.

The plane lurched suddenly. The stewardess fell against a seat back, nearly stumbling into a man's lap. She pushed herself upright and hurried away to buckle herself into her own seat at the front of the plane.

"Please stow all your belongings," her voice came over the intercom. "And make sure your seat belts are securely fastened."

Rochelle's wide eyes locked on mine. "That sounds bad."

The plane jerked again, tossing her against my shoulder. She clenched my arm, terrified.

Turbulence isn't so bad if you've got a pretty girl hanging onto you.

"It's nothing," I told her. "It always feels worse than it really is. The captain knows what he's doing. We'll be fine."

She nodded, but her stricken face was unconvincing. She clutched my arm tighter.

"Tell me about your time in Philadelphia," I suggested, hoping to distract her. "What did you do?"

She shook her head tightly. "No, you talk."

"Well, I was visiting my friend Lucas." I ran through a breezy recap of my time in Philly, trying to keep it light and vague. My steady voice seemed to calm Rochelle's nerves.

An hour later, we were through the worst of the turbulence. When the light came on indicating we could move about the cabin, Rochelle exhaled in relief. She let go of my arm, which was disappointing. The stewardess began the drink service again. Soon, Rochelle and I were on round three.

"It was a wedding I was at." She leaned back and looked thoughtfully at the ceiling. "And it was awful."

"I'm sorry. I don't like weddings at all."

"It wasn't the fact that it was a wedding. The problem was

that I don't think the bride even wanted me there, strange as that sounds."

The plane lurched once more.

"Oh, no. Not this again," Rochelle whispered.

Again, the captain came on. "Hello, everyone. Unfortunately, we're running into another pocket of turbulence. This time, it's looking severe. There's a storm that took an unexpected turn for the worse, and we're experiencing shifts in altitude. We'll be making an emergency landing in Kansas City."

This time, instead of screams, groans echoed through the cabin.

Rochelle nibbled her lips. "Damn."

"I'm sure this doesn't add to your stress."

"Not at all." Her head rolled to the side. "It's okay. All-nighters are a part of college life, right?"

"You're asking me about college life?" I chuckled. "It's been a good seven years since I graduated."

She collected her romance novel from under the seat in front of her and stuffed it into her jacket. My gaze lingered on the bulging pocket. If she was reading romance novels, did that mean romance was lacking in her life? Was she single?

We were quiet as the plane touched down and taxied into the Kansas City airport. Along with a horde of disgruntled travelers, we wheeled our bags into the bright terminal. Through the tall windows, lightning flashed in the sky and rain pummeled the tarmac.

"Well. Here we are." I turned to Rochelle, who was pulling her hair into a high ponytail. Tendrils grazed the back of her neck, and my head spun.

"Yep." She dropped her hands and smiled tightly. "Nice hanging out with you."

"Wait."

She froze, fingers around her suitcase handle. "Uh-huh?"

"I'm going to book a hotel for the night. With this storm, there's no telling when another flight will be available. Care to join me?"

Her tongue flicked out to lick her pink lips. "Oh. No, thank you. I'm fine."

"I didn't mean in that way. I wasn't coming onto you."

Although, truthfully, if she had read the offer that way, I would have been one hundred percent on board.

Her lips turned upward.

"Thank you, but I'll take my chances here. It was nice meeting you..." She stuck out her hand.

"Grant."

"Grant." She turned my name into music.

I took hold of her hand, nearly losing my mind at how silky her skin was. At our touch, electricity traveled up my arm.

"Thanks for the company." She paused. "And for letting me freak out on your arm."

"Anytime."

With a little dip of her head, she turned and sauntered off. I watched her until she disappeared among the bobbing heads, and a groan escaped my chest.

The night was only just getting started, and now I sensed it would be long and boring. But at least it would be over come tomorrow. Until then, I'd do what I could to distract myself with television and takeout.

Doing a quick search on my phone, I found the nearest five-star hotel and called.

"Do you have any rooms available?" I asked the front desk girl.

"I'm sorry, sir. We're all booked."

"Completely?"

"Yes, sir. Due to the storm."

"Thank you." Hanging up, I looked around the terminal. The place was packed. A hundred planes must have made emergency landings here.

Scrolling down the list, I called up two more hotels. Both were also fully booked.

"Shit." One more five-star to go. I'd stay at a four or three if necessary, but honestly I didn't want to.

Though work usually kept me in LA, I sometimes needed to travel for it. Being on the road had never really suited me. So when I did travel, I liked to cheer myself up by staying in the nicest places possible.

At the fourth hotel, I finally struck gold. They had one room left.

"I'll take it."

"Sir, it's the honeymoon suite."

"I don't care. Hell, leave me the champagne and chocolate strawberries or whatever it is you put in there. I need a room."

"Yes, sir."

After giving the receptionist my information, I hung up and wove my way through the crowd. Time to grab a cab.

Throughout the terminal, people lounged in various states. Some stretched out in chairs. Some leaned against walls. It would be a long night, and I felt sorry for anyone who hadn't managed to get a hotel.

Nearly to the escalators, something caught my eye. Doing a double take, I spotted Rochelle. She sat in a chair, her legs hanging over the armrests and her suitcase underneath her seat. She was reading the romance novel again, her corduroy jacket buttoned up to her neck.

Was she spending the night here? It seemed likely.

She didn't notice my approach until I was only a few feet away.

"Hi." Her eyes wide, she put the book down and sat up straight.

"I just booked a hotel."

"Good for you." She blinked a few times, silently asking me what this was about.

"It was the last one I could find. The whole city is filling up quick."

"Ah."

"Come with me. We can share it. It's the honeymoon suite."

She sputtered out a laugh, then sobered. "Wait. You're serious."

I nodded once. "I won't try anything. I promise."

She blushed. "I really am comfortable here."

"We both know that's bullshit. Come with me to the hotel. If there's only one bed, I'll sleep on the couch."

She hesitated, and I could see her gears turning as she tried to decide.

"There could be champagne and chocolate strawberries."

She closed her book. "Well, why didn't you say that in the first place?"

CHAPTER THREE: ADA

I watched as Grant swiped the card and opened the door to the room. The fragrant scent of roses greeted us right away.

Once inside, I gasped lightly. The place was massive. The living area alone was the size of my studio apartment, while off from that was a bedroom and a bathroom. Floor-to-ceiling windows displayed a view of the city. A table in the middle of the room held a bucket with champagne.

"Did you ask them for that?" I parked my suitcase by the door.

"Not at all." He lifted the bottle and studied its label. "As I said, it's the honeymoon suite."

"Anything good?" I asked, nodding at the bottle. Not that I would know. I probably wouldn't have been able to tell thousand-dollar champagne from something you get at a gas station.

"Let's try it out."

Walking past him, I peeked into the bedroom. Rose petals adorned a king-size bed's white comforter. My heart jumped into my throat.

There was only one bed.

But Grant had promised to sleep on the couch. Did I really want that?

I glanced over my shoulder and watched him pop the champagne.

The answer came right away.

No, I didn't want that.

After four days of feeling ignored by my own flesh and blood, which came on the tail end of a semester packed full of classes and waitressing, the last thing I wanted was for Grant to sleep in a different room.

I'd never done hookups. Never had a one-night stand. I always thought that wasn't me. Then again, maybe it had never been the right time or place.

And now definitely felt right. Grant was irritating, sure, but he did more than get under my skin. He lit me up like a Christmas tree, and that was due to his merely looking at me. I wanted to see what he could do when given free rein of my body.

I wanted this. Needed it. The best part was that after tomorrow I would never have to see him again.

"Would you like a glass?" He picked up the two champagne flutes.

"I would love one." I joined him at the coffee table, where

he poured us each a bubbling glass.

Rain struck the windows, creating thousands of little taps. Champagne bubbles fizzed to the tops of our glasses. Our shallow inhales filled the air.

Gazing into Grant's blue eyes, I tapped my glass against his. "To tonight."

"To tonight," he murmured. A shiver ran into my toes.

We drank, and I was surprised at how delicious the champagne was. Crisp and complex, it definitely wasn't a gas station bottle.

"Thank you for joining me." Grant ran his palm down his mouth.

"Thank you for asking me." Something in me squirmed from being this close to him, from wanting him this badly.

I'd never been good with guys, and my instinct was to look away. Instead, I kept my gaze locked onto his.

"So." I batted my eyelashes. "Where are the chocolate strawberries?"

He threw his head back with a laugh. "I can order some, if you like. There's room service. My treat."

Since I'd told him I was a student, he probably knew how broke I was. It didn't matter, though. He'd done me too many favors already by inviting me to the hotel.

"No, thanks. I'm good."

"If you insist. I'll order dinner for you instead." Holding my gaze, he picked up the phone on the coffee table and pressed the button for the dining room. "Hello. We're in the honeymoon suite... Yes. We'll take two filet mignons and whatever your best dessert is."

He raised his eyebrow at me, asking for my approval.

I nodded. Steak sounded delicious. I was probably hungry, but right then I couldn't focus on any sensation except for the hot ache forming between my legs.

Turning away, I took a long drink of champagne. He

finished up the order, but I couldn't hear anything he said. The butterflies in my stomach and the heat in my lower belly drowned out the rest of the world. Could I do this?

Of course I could. It was what I wanted, and if I went to bed without making a move on Grant, I would regret it.

Setting the empty champagne flute on the coffee table, I turned back to him.

"It'll be about an hour." His hands were shoved into his pockets, and his golden-brown hair lay pushed to the side. My fingers ached to run through it.

I swallowed hard. "An hour. What should we do until then?"

He looked at me with the slightest of smiles. "What would you like to do?"

Summoning my inner temptress, the part of me that had never been fully released, I sauntered close to him.

"I don't know." I dropped my voice. "We could think of something, I'm sure."

Grab your copy of Boss Daddy here!

Printed in Great Britain
by Amazon

40060379R00138